Parking the car off the road among the trees, I got out and went slowly over to the house. All the windows were closed; there was no sign of life.

The blank sightless windows of the house stared at me, and suddenly without knowing why, I was frightened. I retreated, moving quickly down the little terraced garden. I noticed that part of an overgrown, weed-strewn flowerbed had been recently dug and hoed.

I stared at it, refusing to recognize it for what it looked like. The patch was about six feet long and three feet wide. Suddenly, hardly aware that I was moving, I was halfway back to the shed. When I reached it I took the spade which was leaning against the wall and went back to the flowerbed at the bottom of the garden.

The spade sank softly into the wet earth and stopped.

I felt horribly cold. Presently I began to shiver again. Then, overcome with an obsession to see all my worst nightmares spring to the most appalling life, I stooped and scraped at the earth until at last I had uncovered a monstrous, distorted, gross object which I only just managed to identify.

It was a human hand.

Fawcett Crest Books
by Susan Howatch:

THE DARK SHORE

THE WAITING SANDS

CALL IN THE NIGHT

THE SHROUDED WALLS

THE DEVIL OF LAMMAS NIGHT

PENMARRIC

APRIL'S GRAVE

CASHELMARA

Susan Howatch

Call in the Night

A FAWCETT CREST BOOK
Fawcett Books, Greenwich, Connecticut

CALL IN THE NIGHT

THIS BOOK CONTAINS THE COMPLETE TEXT OF THE
ORIGINAL HARDCOVER EDITION.

Published by Fawcett Crest Books, CBS Publications, CBS Consumer Publishing, a Division of CBS Inc., by arrangement with Stein and Day Publishers.

Selection of the Bargain Book Club, November 1974

Printed in the United States of America

12   11   10   9   8   7   6   5   4   3

1

It was in the afternoon when the phone call came from Europe, one of those long shimmering afternoons of high summer when the distant reaches of the avenue dissolved into a haze and the heat was locked into the streets by the tall buildings. As soon as I had crawled home from an ill-advised window shopping spree along Fifth Avenue I went to the air conditioner, pressed the switch and stood for a few moments before the fan as I stared out of the window. Eighteen floors below me pedestrians toiled along the pavement and traffic broiled at the intersections; twenty blocks away to the northwest a helicopter prowled through the sky and tip-toed to a landing on the summit of the Pan Am Building. I was reminded of a fastidious fly examining a piece of angel cake.

I turned, moved away from the window and opened the door of the closet which the owners of the apartment hopefully described as a kitchen. There was a bottle of Bitter Lemon in the icebox; underneath the sink was the small bottle of gin which I always kept in readiness against the possibility of unexpected guests, although why I bothered to keep such a thing I don't know since none of my girlfriends had a penchant for alcohol and I had hardly reached the stage of being a secret drinker. However, I had fallen into the habit of keeping an unopened bottle of gin in the apartment ever since the time several months ago when I had been in the embarrassing position of being unable to offer a date anything stronger than ginger ale, and habits, unlike male escorts, are easy to acquire and hard to shake off. Now, because I was so exhausted and felt totally limp with the heat, I seized the gin bottle and poured a minute measure into the glass to join the ice and the Bitter Lemon. I smiled, feeling pleasantly wicked to be drinking alone, and thought how shocked my parents would have been if they could have seen me. Both had been total abstainers, pillars of a very proper New England community in New Hampshire; my father had even refused to grow apples on the small farm where we had lived because he disapproved so strongly of cider.

I sighed, half in irritation, half in regret at my memories. That chapter of my life was closed now, and although I missed my parents and occasionally suffered vague pangs of nostalgia for the New Hampshire countryside, I was in fact thankful to be free of that strict New England upbringing. Even now I sometimes wondered if I were completely free of it. After twenty-eight years in the world and three years in New York City I was still smitten with guilt if I bought clothes which were frivolous rather than useful, and worried myself silly if I didn't have a healthy balance at the bank.

"So *sensible,* darling!" Gina always used to say. "If *only* I could be more like you!"

But she wasn't. Gina was utterly different, so different that I had no idea how we had managed to maintain close contact with one another after our parents' deaths. She was five years younger than I, and so had had five years less of exposure to the New England influences. For a time while she had worked in New York I had conscientiously tried to keep an eye on her, but after a while

6

I gave up. It was much too exhausting, and anyway I had no wish to quarrel with her by criticizing her shortcomings. So we went our separate ways, and later I had my somewhat dubious reward when she went to Hollywood and scribbled reams of rushed letters to me concerning her work and her excessively complicated love life. Evidently my tolerant resignation, which my parents would undoubtedly have judged to be cowardice to tackle a moral issue, had encouraged Gina to cast me for the role of confidante. The mail from California came with great regularity. At first she had tried to phone collect, but I didn't take kindly to that.

"Three minutes only," I told her. "I'm sorry but I'm rather broke at the moment and can't afford any more. I don't want to have to eat yogurt for dinner as well as for lunch."

"But darling, how *can* you be poor!" She sounded so upset at the thought of it that I began to feel touched by her concern. "I mean, you must make such an awful lot of money teaching those terrible children——"

"Not as much as you make in a thirty-second soap commercial," I said with truth, and then felt guilty lest she should think I was being mean, so I encouraged her to talk for ten minutes and postponed buying the *Antony and Cleopatra* album until another time.

However, she took the hint, and after that the letters started to arrive. I began to feel that perhaps I had missed my vocation in life and that I should have been running an advice column for females in distress. "I hardly know what to say," I wrote despairingly in an early letter back to her. "I don't think you find my comments any use to you at all. I can't imagine why you should think that just because I'm five years older than

7

you I have a total, all-enveloping knowledge of human relationships and problems."

"But you're so sane!" cried Gina's pen, weeping purple ink on to pink paper in reply. "So sensible! If you only knew how comforting it is in this mad crazy mixed-up beastly city to have *someone somewhere* who can talk sense and behave normally. . . ."

In fact I think I had become a parent-substitute for her, a symbol, however inaccurate, of the orderly world she could remember from her childhood, and that although nothing would have induced her to return to the discipline of a New England existence, it comforted her to think that it was always there if ever she needed it.

After a few months of this peculiar correspondence, I found I was becoming much fonder of her than I had been when we had both lived in New York; distance lends enchantment. When she came through New York en route to a modeling career in Paris we had a very enjoyable week together, but I could not pretend to myself that I wasn't slightly relieved when the time came for us to part again. I felt like a quiet, placid house in a quiet, tree-lined road of some quiet small town which has suddenly been hit by a tornado, lifted off the ground, spun around three times in mid-air and then dropped back into place with an earth-jarring jolt.

Gina had been six months in Paris on that afternoon in early July when I returned from my window shopping stroll along Fifth Avenue. I had had lunch with an old college friend, and had left my apartment building before the arrival of the mail, which was never delivered before noon on Saturdays. When I returned exhausted at four o'clock I almost forgot to check the mailbox but fortunately I remembered, and there, waiting for me, was the familiar airmail envelope and the familiar dizzy purple-inked handwriting beneath the familiar French stamps. After I had mixed myself my illicit Bitter Lemon, I subsided on to the couch, shook off my shoes and put my feet up. Then with my glass in one hand and Gina's letter in the other I settled down to assume my well-worn rôle of guide, philosopher and friend.

It started in the usual way. According to Gina, this was "just a little note." Sighing with resignation I began to count the pages of whirling purple loops and curls, and then curiosity got the better of me and I went back to the beginning again.

". . . this is just a little note, darling, honestly, as I'm so rushed I'm nearly going out of my mind and I'm supposed to be in three different places at once right now and oh! life's so complicated just trying to fit everything in, and sometimes I wish I was like you, darling, honestly, with your nice steady job and your regular salary and your dear little apartment the size of a dime and your view of midtown Manhattan, and sometimes I really do wish I was back in New York with the luncheonettes and the pizza shops and the bars and the heat that bounces up from the sidewalk to meet you, because although Paris is so glamorous and so exciting and so *soigné*, it does nothing but rain and one does get just a *little* tired of all those dashing French males pinching one's bottom on the Metro. Talking of males, I've just discovered the most enthralling specimen you could ever imagine, and—just for a change—he has absolutely nothing to do with the world of fashion or photography, and he's not even French either, and let's face it, darling, I'm just about due for a change of nationality romance-wise after six months of warding off/egging on would-be Latin lovers. This latest gem is British, but not the bowler-hatted variety or even the Carnaby Street variety either (yes, believe it or not, there *are* other kinds!). His name is Garth Cooper. He seems to be unmarried, but I can't think how he's managed to escape for so long because he's about thirty-five and there's nothing wrong with him, quite the reverse in fact, as I've been discovering recently when we've been out on the town together. In fact that reminds me, we went out together last night and GUESS who we saw! Just guess! You never will, never in a million years—Warren Mayne! And if you'll believe it, he came right up and kissed me as if he was still my fiancé. Some people have an awful nerve, don't they? I was embarrassed to pieces and didn't even dare look at Garth but afterwards he seemed amused and said it looked as if Warren had come to work in Paris so that he could get in touch with me again. Of course I denied it, but I *did* wonder. Oh, it's just too much of Warren if he has followed me to Paris! It'll make life so horribly complicated and I just can't bear it, it's complicated enough already, and sometimes I can't help wishing you were here to sort it out for me—incidentally hasn't school finished for the summer yet? What are you doing about a vacation? Rake those surplus dollars out of your bulging bank account and buy yourself a round trip excursion flight to Paris! Must rush, darling, no more now, love and take care and all the rest, GINA."

I sighed again, sipped my gin and reflected what a mysterious thing sex appeal is. Gina and I look rather alike—or at least we used to before Gina took to false eyelashes and the hollow-cheeked look—but she obviously has a certain mysterious quality which I lack. I really can't believe the mystery rests on false eyelashes alone so I suppose some extraordinary fusion of the hereditary quirks of our very ordinary parents must be responsible. Whatever it is, it never seems very fair. But then unless one is a complete ingenue one hardly expects life to be fair; I had long ago resigned myself to that basic truth so I was always cross when I caught myself behaving like an ingenue again and envying Gina her good luck.

As if, I thought disgusted with myself, I even wanted to be a model. She was welcome to it all, Paris, men and mink coats! I was perfectly happy with my Shakespeare records and my friends and the Metropolitan museum on Sundays; I had a job I liked, an apartment of my own, and perhaps, if I were careful with my saving and my raise came through shortly, a shining little red Volkswagen. . . .

After day-dreaming for several minutes of stepping casually into my very own car as the doorman held open the door for me with an admiring smile, I roused myself, found pen and paper and sat down again to consider a reply. I always found Gina's letters easier to answer if I made the effort to write when her initial impression was still clear in my mind. To write a guide-philosopher-friend letter in cold blood after an interval of several days was much too turgid a task to face.

"My dear Gina," I began, scratching away nimbly at the paper. "How you do ramble on, although I'm sure I'm just as bad myself sometimes. Here are my comments in chronological order: 1) You know darn well you'd rather be in Paris in the rain than in a ninety-degree-ninety-percent-humidity New York, so don't ask me for sympathy on *that* issue. 2) If the Metro is such a danger spot for the more vulnerable parts of your anatomy, catch a bus and sit down at once. 3) I don't trust this thirty-five year old Englishman. Why should he be (apparently) floating around Paris with money to burn? Also, what do you mean when you say he 'seems' to be unmarried. That sounds as if you really think he might be married. If he is, say a tender goodbye now, and then maybe I won't have to offer you my shoulder to cry on long distance in six months' time, when he suddenly strikes a noble pose and decides to go back to his wife. 4) Bad luck about meeting Warren again. However, if you don't want to see him in the future, there's one quite simple remedy. Tell him so. 5) I'd love to come to Paris and see you but am just about to get my little red car which I told you about when you were here last winter. Maybe next year? I'm not having a very ambitious vacation this year, just a week in Boston with Sue and her husband and a week in Martha's Vineyard at Nancy's cottage there . . ."

I paused to reread what I had written before continuing my own news, and swallowed the last of my drink. I was just picking up my pen again to resume the letter when the phone rang.

Reaching backwards I grabbed the receiver and knocked over my empty glass. "Yes?" I said confused, picking up my glass and retrieving my writing-pad which had slid off my knees to the floor. "Hello?"

"Miss Claire Sullivan, please."

"Speaking," I said dimly, puzzled by the unfamiliar man's voice and the hum of the long distance wire.

"Miss Sullivan, this is London, England. Will you accept a call, please, from a Miss Gina Sullivan who wishes to reverse the charges?"

I was so surprised that I even forgot to be annoyed at Gina's further attempt to call collect. "London?" I said in amazement. "London, England?"

"Yes, madam. Shall I—" He paused politely.

There was no mistaking the British courtesy. Or the British accent.

"Yes," I said rapidly. "Yes, I'll take the call. Thank you."

"Go ahead, please, caller."

"Gina?" I said at once incredulously. "Gina, what are you doing in—"

But she was already talking, not listening to me, her voice high-pitched and breaking with panic, her breath coming in sobs and gasps, and as I listened her terror communicated itself to me until I too was rigid with her fear.

"Oh Claire, Claire, please come," she was sobbing. "Please come, Claire. Oh Claire, I'm in such dreadful terrible trouble I don't know what to do—Claire, you just have to come, please, please—I don't know what to do—"

"Gina listen! Where are you, for God's sake? What's happened? What—Gina, are you there? Gina—"

But there was nothing there any more, just that long empty silence, and then across a distance of four thousand miles I heard the soft stealthy click of the receiver being replaced.

2

The buzz of the disconnected wire produced a reaction from me of stupefied disbelief. I stared at the silent phone and listened to the dull *purr* as if I were completely paralyzed, and then at last I pulled myself together, called the operator, and asked for the international circuits.

"I was speaking to London—I was cut off—" I couldn't think clearly; I heard myself stumble over the questions the operator asked. "No—no, I don't know the number in London . . . yes, if you could please trace the call for me . . ."

I hung up, waited, mixed myself another gin. At last, just as I thought I could bear waiting no longer, the phone rang again.

"The call came from 16, Hereford Mansions, London W.8.," said the operator sedately. "Number: Kensington 21272. The number is listed under the name of a Mr. Eric Jantzen, that's J-A-N-T-Z-E-N. Shall I try the number for you?"

"Please." My pencil whispered across the paper, recording the information she had given me.

"Whom are you calling, please?"

"Gina Sullivan." I spelled it.

"One moment, please."

I waited, listening. Presently I heard the dialing, followed by the sound of the bell ringing far away.

"Trying to connect you," said the operator.

"Thank you."

It went on ringing.

"Still trying to connect you," said the operator.

"Thank you."

A long pause.

"I'm sorry," said the operator. "There's no reply. Can I try the number again for you later?"

I couldn't think what to say. At last I said: "No, thank you, but could you check the address of the call again? My sister has never mentioned anyone called Eric Jantzen and I want to be quite sure there was no mistake."

"Call you back," said the operator, impersonal as an automaton, and hung up.

I replaced the receiver and sat staring into my glass. Supposing I kept trying the number and still got no reply? What was I to do? I'll wait till midnight, I thought and then if I haven't managed to contact Gina or if she hasn't called back. . . . My scalp prickled. What was I to do then? It would be no good calling the police of the local precinct about something which had happened in London. And if I called the police in London, spoke to Scotland Yard . . . I tried to imagine the conversation.

"My sister called me from London just now," I would say. "She sounded very frightened and hysterical. Then we were cut off and the receiver was replaced and now I can't re-establish contact with her. Could you check the address of this apartment belonging to Eric Jantzen and see if she's all right?"

Did one ask Scotland Yard to give reassurance about one's relatives? I mentally tried a more dramatic approach. "I'm afraid something dreadful has happened to my sister—we were cut off in the middle of our conversation and it sounded as if someone had silenced her. . . .

But that wasn't true. Gina hadn't mentioned that she was in danger, only 'in trouble.' If she had been interrupted by someone who had silenced her and replaced the receiver, she had given no indication of it. There had been no scream, no gasp of horror, only the hysteria and sheer panic which I, perhaps mistakenly, had interpreted as a hysteria born of fear. I rephrased my approach to Scotland Yard and imagined the subsequent conversation.

"I've had a very disturbing phone call from the apartment of a Mr. Eric Jantzen," I would say. "My sister was hysterical and sounded immensely frightened—I think

15

it's vital that the call should be investigated—"

And Scotland Yard would interrupt: "What was your sister doing in London? How well did she know this Eric Jantzen?"

"I don't know, but she was friends with an Englishman called Garth Cooper."

"You say your sister's a model by profession?" Scotland Yard would say instantly. "Young—smart—presumably attractive to men?"

"Yes, but—"

"Isn't it likely that she was hysterical as the result of a crisis which was possibly brought on by her relationship with either or both of these two men?"

"Well, yes, but—"

"Did she actually say she was afraid? Or in danger?"

"No, but—"

"What were her exact words?"

I winced. I didn't have to imagine Scotland Yard's comment on that particular phrase. I was just wondering if I should call them anyway, when the phone rang again. It was the operator confirming Jantzen's name and address. I told her I had changed my mind, and asked her to try the number again for me in an hour's time. After I had replaced the receiver, I had a brainwave, and going over to the bureau on the other side of the room I got my writing case and found the phone number of Gina's apartment in Paris. Gina shared the apartment with another American girl, whom I had never met, called Candy-Anna; I particularly remembered the eccentric hybrid of a first name, although I had long since forgotten the second. Presently I was talking to the international information department again, and placing yet another call to Europe.

This time I was more successful. A voice as languid as

16

melting maple syrup answered the ringing phone and breathed a tingling hello into the mouthpiece.

"Go ahead, caller," the operator said.

"Candy-Anna?"

"Ye-es," said the voice, sagging a little with the realization that I wasn't an escort calling for a date. "Who's this?"

"Gina's sister Claire in New York. I—"

"Well, *hi!* I've heard *so* much about you! Gina was saying only yesterday—"

"Yes, I'm trying to find her." My interruption was hardly very adroit but she appeared not to notice my abruptness. "Do you know whereabouts in London she is, please?"

"Why, how clever of you to know she's in London! She only decided yesterday to—"

"Do you know where she's staying there?"

"Well, no—no, not really . . . She traveled over with a friend of hers, a wonderful, wonderful man who you'd just love to meet—"

"Garth Cooper?"

"Why, you *know* him! Isn't he the most—"

"No, I haven't met him. Do you know where he lives in London?"

"Gee, no—is it important? Gina'll be back on Monday —she was only going for the weekend and she said—"

"Did she ever mention the name Eric Jantzen to you?"

"Eric who? Honey, I just don't remember! If you knew how many wonderful men Gina has absolutely panting on our doorstep—" Sour grapes tinged the maple syrup sweetness briefly and was gone. "I'm sorry I just can't remember—honestly. I don't *think* she ever mentioned an Eric, but it's just possible I might have forgotten. I forget terribly easily. My memory's just the

17

most hopeless thing you could ever imagine . . . Say, how's New York? What time is it there? Tell me all about it!"

Not at three dollars a minute, I thought with wry amusement, but I said politely that it was afternoon in New York and the weather was fine and I was so grateful for her help and hoped to meet her one day. Having escaped from the conversation as gracefully as possible I got up and moved restlessly over to the window.

I simply did not know what to do. I glanced at my watch. It was five-thirty, ten-thirty in England. In half an hour the operator would try the Jantzen number again. I at least had till six o'clock to decide what to do if I were unable to make contact with Gina.

I tried to consider the situation quite dispassionately. What did I really think had happened? If I were honest I had to admit I believed Gina had got into some sort of emotional tangle with Garth Cooper and Eric Jantzen. I knew from past experience that Gina had an enormous talent for tying her love life up into the most preposterous knots. She had probably gone to London with Cooper and then discovered from Eric Jantzen, whoever he was, that Cooper was married after all. In her shock she had characteristically dramatized the situation by believing her heart to be utterly broken for all time, and carried away by a sense of tragedy had made the phone call to tell me what trouble she was in.

Then why had she hung up in the middle of the conversation?

I worried over the question until the phone rang again at six o'clock.

"There's still no reply from the London number," said the operator. "Shall I call again at seven?"

I made a spur of the moment decision. "No," I said.

18

"Could you please place a call for me to Scotland Yard?"

I suspected that by this time even the automaton of an operator was beginning to doubt my sanity.

"Scotland Yard, London?"

"Yes," I said. "The police."

"Person to person?"

"No, no—anyone will do. I want to report something."

"Call you back," said the operator in the kind of voice one uses to the mentally disturbed, and left me listening once more to the dull buzz of a severed connection.

I began to rehearse my story again and tried to suppress a feeling of mounting nervousness and panic. When I was finally called upon to tell my story some minutes later I found myself, much to my fury, stammering over my carefully rehearsed words while my face burned with my embarrassment.

Fortunately the policeman at the other end of the wire, Detective-Inspector Fowles, listened and commented courteously enough and asked me the right questions to straighten out my confused story. When I asked in desperation at last if the police would be able to help, he was reassuringly placid.

"Yes, we'll send someone round to make an inquiry at the Jantzen flat," he said. "Don't you worry, we'll look into it straight away. If there's been any funny business going on we'll sort it out and find out what's happening to your sister."

"Can you let me know any news as soon as possible? I realize these phone calls must be very expensive, but I'd really appreciate it if—"

"Yes, of course, Miss Sullivan. Now I have a note of your number here, don't I? I'll give you a ring myself as soon as the report comes through and I have some news for you."

I thanked him gratefully, replaced the receiver and then leaned back on the couch and closed my eyes. I felt exhausted. After a while I went to the kitchen and half heartedly tried to cook myself some supper, but I found I could eat nothing.

I walked restlessly about the room, stood by the window, stared out at the Pan Am Building and the other giant buildings. Another helicopter landed and departed. Seven o'clock came. Lights were pinpricking the dusk; night-time New York was coming alive, and far below me on the Avenue I could see the red tail lights of the cars as they cruised *en masse* to the midtown restaurants and the glitter of Broadway. Soon it was eight o'clock. Then nine. Twice I nearly picked up the phone in an agony of impatience, but managed to restrain myself; the man at Scotland Yard would call back. It was senseless calling him when he might not yet have the news I wanted. I was just making myself another cup of coffee shortly before eleven-thirty when the ring of the phone made me spill boiling water over the floor.

"Hello?" I said nervously into the receiver. "Claire Sullivan speaking."

It was Scotland Yard, Detective-Inspector Fowles again. My knees were unsteady suddenly; I had to sit down.

"Miss Sullivan, I'm afraid we have no real news of your sister but all seems to be quite in order so perhaps no news is good news. Mr. Jantzen had invited her to have a drink with him, but he was delayed and couldn't keep the engagement—he tried to contact her to cancel the evening but couldn't get in touch with her. He was completely unaware that your sister had ever been in the flat."

"But—" I was confused. "How did she get in if he wasn't there?"

20

"He suggested that she might have come with a friend of hers, a Mr. Cooper. Apparently this Mr. Cooper has a key to the Jantzen flat."

Somewhere far away at the back of my mind I was conscious of a slight unreasoning stab of fear.

"Did you check with Mr. Cooper?" I said uneasily.

"We haven't been able to contact him so far, but I shouldn't worry too much, if I were you, Miss Sullivan. Apparently your sister came over from Paris with this Mr. Cooper—"

"Yes," I said. "I know."

"I expect they've gone out on the town tonight—your sister's probably having the time of her life, and enjoying every minute of her visit!" He sounded comforting, reassuring; I could tell that he himself was convinced nothing was wrong. "Look, I'll tell you what I think happened—she and Cooper went to his friend's flat for a drink and had a tiff about something. Maybe he pretended to walk out. Well, you know these young girls—and your sister probably enjoyed a spot of drama now and again. She put through her call to you to weep on your shoulder—and then lo and behold he turns up again all ready to apologize and they go off together quite happily as if nothing had ever happened. You mark my words, you'll have a call from her tomorrow saying she's sorry she gave you such a fright."

All I could say was: "Supposing she doesn't call?"

"Well, if she doesn't . . ." He paused to consider this remote possibility. "Give it till Monday and then check up to see if she got back to Paris safely. If she didn't and if there's still no word from her, then get in touch with me again."

"All right," I said slowly. "All right, I will. And thank you very much for all the trouble you've taken."

"Not at all, Miss Sullivan. Don't mention it."

We said goodbye, he very cordial and friendly, I stilted with anxiety and uneasiness.

Presently I sat down on the couch and remained there for a long while, but the more I told myself that it was foolish to go on worrying, the more worried I became. The thought of waiting another forty-eight hours until Monday without doing anything except wile away the time was not a pleasant thought. At last, in an agony of indecision and nervousness I got up, went over to my purse and had a look at the balance in my checkbook. After a little simple arithmetic with the balance in my savings account I sat thinking for a long while. I was remembering the car again, my little red Volkswagen waiting patiently for me to save up the money to buy it. I thought of the trips I had planned, the luxury of excursions out of town to the beach in summer without the tedium of the long subway ride, the six-week expedition to the West I had visualized during next year's summer vacation.

I thought for a long time.

"Well," I said aloud to myself at last, "perhaps it would all have been rather extravagant. And everyone says that keeping a car in Manhattan is more of a liability than an asset. I can wait a little longer for that sort of extravagance. And I always did want to go to Europe."

Having reached my decision I felt much better. I went to bed, snatched a few hours' sleep, and as soon as I awoke next morning I dialed Pan Am to inquire how soon they could offer me a seat on a flight from New York to London.

Fate then took a hand in the proceedings; I discovered

that because it was the height of the summer tourist season at that time, all the planes were fully booked on the flights to London. I put my name down on several lists, and then, nearly beside myself with frustration, I paused to consider the situation. It was now Sunday morning. Even if I got a flight that same day I would hardly be able to reach London before Gina left England to return to France—assuming, of course, that Gina was safe and well. That being the case it would be more sensible for me to try to obtain a flight not to London, but to Paris. I went back to the phone again and eventually, by a stroke of luck, found there was a cancellation on a TWA flight to Paris on Monday. Having made my reservation and committed myself positively to my decision to go to Europe I was at last able to relax a little, but there was too much to do to enable me to relax for long. I set out for Forty-second Street to exchange a check for a ticket to Paris, and as I walked I found myself again thinking of Gina, her suave Englishman Garth Cooper, Candy-Anna saying in her carefully preserved southern drawl: "Such a wonderful, wonderful man. . . ."

I began to be nervous once more. I could hardly reach the airlines' building at Forty-second Street quickly enough.

Half an hour later with my ticket safely in my purse I returned home and tried to prepare for my journey in an organized manner, but I found I was still too distraught to conform to any careful routine. I checked my passport and smallpox vaccination certificate; eternally optimistic, I had always kept both valid. The dreary task of packing lay before me. Finally when my suitcases were closed I called a couple of friends to tell them that I had decided to take a surprise trip to Europe. Both friends were suitably amazed. I began to wonder vaguely

23

if I was indeed demented, but pushed the thought out of my mind as I sent a cable to Gina's apartment in Paris to announce my arrival.

Perhaps, I thought, determined to be optimistic and believe that all was well, perhaps Gina would be at the airport to meet me.

But somehow at the back of my mind I remained uneasily convinced that no one would be there when my plane touched down at Orly. I started to worry again, worrying all through Sunday night, and then at last it was Monday and I was rushing to my bank at nine to buy travelers' checks before taking a cab out to Kennedy to catch the morning flight. Fortunately all went well; there were no delays, no last minute disasters, and within forty-eight hours of Gina's phone call from London I was on my way to Europe to find her.

The flight seemed endless. For hour after hour the plane seemed suspended in a blue vacuum, and at last the time difference between Europe and America manifested itself in a spectacular sunset and an early twilight. By the time we reached Paris it was night, although my watch told me that in New York it was still late afternoon. I thought of the long avenues dissolving into a heat-haze, the stifling side-walks, the drone of a million air conditioners, and suddenly that was far away on the other side of the world and the plane was beginning its long downward path to the runway and French soil.

I roused myself from the torpor of the long flight, put away my book, forgot to feel nervous. Below me I could see lights, European lights, pinpricking the darkness of the summer night, and my excitement was such that for a moment I forgot Gina altogether. The plane sank lower and lower; the lights stretched as far as I could see. Presently I saw the lights of the airport, and as the plane sank still lower to meet them I remembered to fasten my safety belt. Within a quarter of an hour the plane had landed and I was stepping out into a new and different land.

My excitement rose in a crescendo and then ebbed. I felt alone, foreign, shy. I did have a slight knowledge of French so I was not completely at a loss but the rapid cross-fire of conversation around me was far removed from the simple phrases I had learned at school. Feeling very lost and helpless I filtered through Customs and Immigration and was directed by dual-language signs to the place where I could get a bus to the terminal. I hung back, hoping in spite of myself that there would be some sign of Gina, but there was no face I knew; I remained a stranger among strangers and the airport continued to seem cold and impersonal.

After a delay I managed to cash a traveler's check, and was able to pay my fare and board the bus. My second stage of the journey began; the bus roared through the Parisian suburbs, over cobbled streets, past outdoor cafés and shabby houses. And then suddenly the shabbiness was gone and there were wide boulevards, illuminated vistas, floodlit buildings, incredibly familiar landmarks. We seemed to drive through the middle of the city, and soon my excitement was such that I forgot I was alone and thought only that this was Paris and I, Claire Sullivan, was seeing it all with my own eyes.

I reached the terminal, found my luggage again, hailed a waiting cab.

"*Numéro vingt-deux, Rue St. Thomasine, s'il vous plaît.*"

The driver nodded, assuming an expression of what I supposed was typical Parisian *ennui*. We shot off like a bullet from a gun, bounced over cobbles, screeched to a halt at an intersection. Finally as we cannoned forward again I became adjusted to this spastic form of transport and instead began to feel nervous in case my cable had failed to reach Gina's apartment.

But it had arrived safely. After I had paid the driver and left the cab I found my way into the apartment building with my luggage and shut myself in a small but modern elevator. Gina lived on the third floor. On emerging into the passage I couldn't find a light and had to strike a match, but at last I was outside the right door and reading Gina's name above Candy-Anna's on the name slot.

I was conscious of immense weariness mingled with relief. I rang the bell, waited, and presently the door opened and I was facing a slim willowy girl with honey-blonde hair and limpid blue eyes.

"Well, he*llo* there!" said Candy-Anna, effortlessly hospitable. "Welcome to Europe! It's just wonderful to see you but I hope you're not going to be terribly disappointed. Gina must have decided to prolong that weekend in London—she didn't come back last night after all and I just haven't the remotest idea where she is. . . ."

3

"Who is this man Garth Cooper?" I said. "Have you meet him?"

Half an hour had passed since my arrival, and we were sitting drinking Swiss coffee in the large dishevelled living room. Candy-Anna had been pardonably curious about the suddenness of my trip to Europe and my concern for Gina, but I am not naturally inclined to confide in complete strangers so I had edited and omitted large sections of the story.

"Gina's been pressing me to come to Europe for a vacation, so I decided I would," I had said. "I had a phone call from London on Saturday night in which she sounded very odd, to say the least, but when I called her back I couldn't get in touch with her. That was when I called you to try and find out why she was in London and who she went with."

"Well, she went with Garth," Candy-Anna had answered. "But it wasn't just a wild lost weekend together—my, but you mustn't think that!" Her limpid eyes assumed a carefully cultivated expression of innocence. "Garth was going back to London after being in Paris on business and Gina decided to go too, just for the weekend and to see a bit of England. But I guess the weekend must have been a real blast and she decided to stay on.

Why was her phone call to you so odd? You don't think anything's happened to her, do you?"

"She just didn't seem like herself." I had finished my cup of coffee, and then asked my question about Garth Cooper. "I believe you said on the phone that you'd met him," I added, remembering. "What kind of man is he, do you think?"

But I might have known Candy-Anna would be quite incapable of giving a straight answer to such a question.

"Garth? Why, he's just a wonderful, wonderful person! We both absolutely love him to pieces—"

"Yes," I said, trying not to sound impatient, "but what does he do? Why was he in Paris? Does he live in London?"

"My, I've no idea! I guess he must. But I think he has a small place in Paris too—I remember him saying he was always traveling back and forth between the two places . . . So glamorous!" She sighed. "Imagine living and working in London *and* Paris—"

"Yes," I said again, digging my nails into the palms of my hands. "But what does he *do*?"

Candy-Anna frowned for a moment, probably from the effort of mobilizing unused machinery for thought. "Well, gee," she said at last, vaguely surprised, "isn't that the strangest thing? I've just no idea at all."

"Did he seem rich?"

"Oh *yes*! He took cabs everywhere and never used the metro. And he and Gina went to simply wonderful places to eat and did marvellously glamorous things like going to the opera and the theatre. It was lovely for Gina! I was so happy for her."

I had my doubts about that, but kept them to myself. "How long has Gina known him?"

"Oh . . . about six weeks, I guess. But he hasn't been

28

in Paris for the whole of that time. He was here all last week and they saw each other nearly every night. Then on Friday night they took off for London together."

"I suppose you don't know when he himself is scheduled to come back to Paris?"

"Gee, no! I've no idea. It could be that he'll stay in London for a while now. I just don't know."

I wondered what to do. It was beginning to look as if I should take a plane to London as quickly as possible, find this man Cooper and ask him point blank what had happened to Gina. But then . . . I sighed. I was no doubt being melodramatic and foolish. In all probability Gina was hopelessly involved with him by this time and had no intention of returning to Paris while her romance was flourishing so successfully in London. She wouldn't thank me for interfering. I began to feel as if I had made a complete fool of myself. Against Scotland Yard's advice I had taken a melodramatic view of the phone call and now I was taking an equally melodramatic and misguided approach to Gina's continuing absence from home. I was just telling myself bitterly that it would have been more sensible to have remained in New York instead of rushing across the Atlantic Ocean like a lunatic, when the phone rang.

We both jumped.

"It's Gina," I said at once. "It must be. She's back."

Candy-Anna grabbed the receiver. "Hello?"

I leaned forward on the edge of the couch, my limbs aching, and saw her eyes widen with surprise. "Why, Warren! How are you? What? No, she's not here right now—she's not back yet. Yes, that's right. . . . No, I haven't heard from her—"

I interrupted sharply. "Is that Warren Mayne, Gina's

ex-fiancé?" I was remembering Gina's letter which had reached my apartment shortly before the phone call.

"Just a moment, honey," she said into the receiver, and then to me: "Yes, it is—do you know him?"

"Can I speak to him, please?"

"Sure." She was surprised. She turned her attention back to the receiver. "Honey, just guess who's here wanting a word with you! Someone out of your past!" And having fulfilled her obligation to be mysterious and tantalizing she handed the phone over to me with a dazzling smile and reached out for another cigarette.

"Warren?" I said quickly. "This is Claire Sullivan, Gina's—"

"Claire!" He was amazed. And suddenly I could see him, very young and clean cut, his fair hair too short, his serious face pleasantly ugly, his brown eyes shining with affection like those of a well-trained spaniel. Gina had led him a terrible dance the previous year in New York; I had spent most of our meetings feeling sorry for him.

"Yes!" I said, smiling in spite of my anxiety. "Yes, it really is me! How are you, Warren? I had heard from Gina that you were in Paris now."

"She mentioned me?" He was touchingly gratified. "Yes, I'm working for an American company with offices here. It's—" He stopped, as if halted by the realization that I should be in Manhattan and not in Europe at all. "Well, I'll be darned!" he exclaimed. "Gina didn't mention you were vacationing here! I didn't know you were in Paris!"

"Neither does Gina. It's all an involved story and I seem to have got into a muddle, to say the least. I'm told Gina's in London with someone called Garth Cooper."

Candy-Anna clapped her hand over her mouth and shook her head frantically, but she was too late. There was a sharp gasp from the other end of the wire, and as I blushed scarlet in my confusion Warren shouted: "What! Cooper? Gina went to London with Garth Cooper? Why, she told me—"

I inwardly cursed myself for not having the presence of mind to foresee the situation. "They weren't together," I said helplessly, making things worse. "They just took the same plane."

"Well, where is she now, for Pete's sake? Why isn't she back? My God, if I'd known that Cooper was going to London with her—"

"Warren, you must excuse me, but I don't really understand any of this myself. I've only just arrived and I'm not at all sure what's been happening as far as Gina's concerned. Could we meet tomorrow and talk about all this? I'm a little confused."

"Well, I'm not." He was obviously still beside himself with rage. "It's all as clear as daylight to me. That damned Englishman flashed his money around and invited her to come with him on a guided tour of London! My God, if I ever see him again—"

"Perhaps if we could talk about it tomorrow, Warren, I—"

"Breakfast? Lunch?" he asked quickly.

"How about lunch?" I suggested, hoping I'd hear from Gina before then.

"Fine. I'll stop by at your place at noon," he said furiously and slammed down the receiver.

"Oh dear," I said ineffectually. "Why on earth did I have to be so stupid? Now I've made the situation worse for Gina than it was already."

Candy-Anna was reassuring. "Gina doesn't care about

31

Warren anyway. She'd be glad for the excuse to get rid of him forever." Her eyes held a hint of speculation. I guessed she would be glad too, but for different reasons.

"I must go to bed," I said exhausted. "I feel worn out. I apologize for descending on you like this, Candy-Anna, and putting you to such inconvenience . . ."

I was assured that I was very welcome and that there was no need to apologize.

In the end I slept in Gina's bed with Gina's familiar belongings strewn around me. Candy-Anna breathed peacefully across the room, but I slept lightly, half-expecting the phone to ring again with news, good or bad, from London. But there was no news and no phone call and when I opened my eyes at last it was eight o'clock and the sun was streaming through the slanting slats of the Venetian blinds.

Warren arrived punctually at noon. Candy-Anna had left earlier for a business appointment ("Modeling engines, honey—would you believe? I have to pose with a truck and a baby elephant.") and I was on my own when the bell rang. I went across to the door to open it.

Warren looked exactly the same as when I had last seen him. He was, I suppose, nearer my age than Gina's but I always thought of him as being at least five years my junior. When Gina had come to New York after our parents' deaths she had studied art for a while in Manhattan and had met Warren while they were both going through the long-haired Greenwich Village stage. Unfortunately for Warren, Gina had outgrown the phase more quickly than he had, and after finding success as a model in New York she had moved away, first to Hollywood and then to Paris, and there had been copious stormy scenes with the diamond engagement ring being pushed back and forth and finally discarded altogether. I could not help feeling Warren had been unlucky, since he was in his own way extremely eligible and plenty of girls would have been very anxious to catch him. He came from a good family; his father was in the diplomatic service in Washington. He was not particularly cultured or intellectual, but then neither was Gina; I thought it would have been a good match, but Gina had thought otherwise, and had gone off to fresh fields and new pastures in pursuit of what she had considered to be a more glamorous existence.

"It's good to see you again," he said, offering me his hand and smiling his bright naive smile. "I'm sorry I was so rude on the phone last night, but I was upset."

"It was nice of you to come around," I said politely, "I was hoping that perhaps you'd be able to tell me what's been going on."

"I was hoping you were going to tell *me*," said Warren. He glanced at his watch. "Look, there's a small restaurant just down the road—why don't we go out and get something to eat there? I'll bet there's nothing in the ice-box here except yogurt. Models never eat anything."

I had naturally assumed that we would go out to lunch, so his bland assumption that I might have been prepared to cook him a meal rather took me aback. I said hastily that I would be very interested in trying a French restaurant, and together we left the apartment and went into the cool fresh air of the street outside.

I caught my breath. Looking down the road I could see the Seine and beyond that, further up the river, the shining splendor of the Eiffel Tower. The sky was blue, the sun warm, but there was little humidity. New York seemed a million years away.

"How wonderful it is to be in Paris!" I exclaimed

33

spontaneously. "I can't think why I never made the effort to come before."

Warren smiled condescendingly. "It does seem exciting at first, doesn't it?" he said in the indulgent tone of a father talking to a child. "I felt the same too, when I arrived."

I could have murdered him.

However, my irritation ebbed when we reached the little restaurant and sat outside on the pavement under a striped umbrella. We ordered steaks and wine and then relaxed in our chairs to wait.

"They'll take hours," said Warren. "French service is the slowest in the world."

"That doesn't matter," I said firmly, putting him in his place, and to change the subject I began: "Now about Gina—"

"Exactly," said Warren with alacrity. "Look, what's going on? How did you know she was in London with Cooper? What did she tell you? Did she say she'd be back in Paris to meet you? Why isn't she here? Where is she?"

I began the weary task of explanations. I told him everything, partly because I knew him well, partly because he was obviously as worried about Gina as I was, and partly because I felt I had to discuss the situation with someone. He listened intelligently enough to begin with, but after a while I sensed he was rapidly becoming too jealous to concentrate on what I was saying.

"So there it is," I concluded at last, ignoring the sulky droop of his mouth and the introspective look in his eyes. "I don't know where she is or what's happened to her, and I'm worried—perhaps unreasonably." I hesitated and then asked the question I had put to Candy-

Anna the previous evening: "What kind of person is this man Garth Cooper?"

The waiter arrived with our order and interrupted us, but I did not have to repeat my question. As soon as the waiter had left us Warren said angrily: "Well, he's English to start with. I never trust the English. The biggest fallacy in the world is to think they're just like us because they speak the same language—they're not like us at all."

I made an effort to avoid an argument on the subject of racial prejudice. "You mean you don't trust Cooper?"

"I never trust the English," said Warren obstinately. "You can never tell what they're thinking. They're always so polite, so cool and so damned charming, and then suddenly you find they're all set to stab you in the back. Cooper tried to give me the impression that he wasn't really interested in Gina at all and that he wished me well—and then what happens? I find he's taken her off to London for the weekend! Well, if that isn't two-faced double-dealing, damn it, I don't know what is—"

"But as far as I can gather they were merely traveling together—"

"Look," said Warren. "You don't seriously think they're going to shake hands at the London airport and go their separate ways, do you? Why do you think she went to London?"

"It's an interesting city," I said annoyed by his eagerness to read guilt in what might well have been an innocent situation. "Why shouldn't she have wanted to see it with or without Garth Cooper?"

"Because Gina's all tied up emotionally with this damned man Cooper. He's a rich, successful business-man of about thirty-five. He's sophisticated—he knows his way around Paris and I'll bet he knows his way around London too. He's the sort of man women drool over as soon as he enters a room, while men ask each other what the hell he has that they don't have. Gina, as usual, has gone into the whole business with her eyes tight shut—she never even stopped to ask herself if he was married or what kind of a background he had—"

"You mean he's the playboy type?"

"I mean he's a womanizer. He knows I came to France to be with Gina and yet that didn't stop him from taking her out on the town and spending all that money—"

I was becoming a little tired of Mr. Cooper's money. "But Warren," I said reasonably, "Gina chose to go out with him, didn't she? And you're not her fiancé any more, if you'll forgive my saying so. If she chose to go out with him it's bad luck for you, but in Cooper's eyes she doesn't belong to you any more than she belongs to him."

"She's infatuated with him," said Warren obstinately. "It's me she really loves."

I was silent. It was impossible for me to say that this was highly unlikely.

"If I can only get her away from Cooper—if I could only persuade her to notice me again . . ." He refilled his glass of wine; he was drinking much too quickly, ". . . she'd come back to me," he said. "I know it. That's why I'm here. I got my father to pull some strings and fix me this job for a year. It's not well paid but at least I'm in Paris near Gina—if only Cooper would stay in England and leave me alone with her, I know I just know, that everything would work out all right."

I almost said: "If it wasn't Cooper it would be some other man," but I checked myself. I had learned long ago that it's no good arguing with someone in love. "What *is* Garth Cooper's business?" I said after a moment. "Do you know what he does?"

"Sure. He deals in china and glass, some of it antique, some of it modern, but all of it valuable. He's involved with the importing and exporting of special lines of china and glass between England and France."

"His main office is in London, I suppose?"

"Yes, but he has a small base here in Paris. He told me it's an office-cum-apartment, where he stays as well as works when he's here. It's not a big firm—he's his own boss."

"Does he have any partners?"

He looked at me in surprise. "But I thought you knew? You mentioned the name when you told me where Gina's call came from. You mean to say you didn't realize all along who Cooper's partner is?"

"Not Eric Jantzen!"

"No," said Warren, "his wife. Cooper's partner is Eric Jantzen's wife Lilian."

It transpired that Warren had never met either of the Jantzens and that his knowledge of their existence was derived solely from his meeting with Cooper and Gina during the previous week.

"I arrived in Paris a month ago," he said. "It took me some time to trace Gina, and then just as I had managed to discover her address I met her by chance in one of the restaurants on the Champs Elysées. That was last Tuesday. She was with Cooper but I went up to her just the same—Cooper was very pleasant, or seemed to be, and asked me to join them for a drink, so I accepted and sat talking with them both for about twenty minutes. Or at least Gina didn't talk much; it was Cooper who carried the conversation—he went all out to give the impression that his relationship with Gina was a very casual one, but I'm not a fool and I wasn't taken in by what he said. And when I called up Gina later—" He winced. "We had several rows over the phone. I soon realized that Cooper had misled me, and that in fact she was heavily involved with him. On Thursday I asked her if I could see her over the weekend and she said she was going to Brittany sightseeing with Candy-Anna. So I call Monday night to ask her how she made out and you tell me she went to London with Cooper."

I was silent, thinking of Gina, wondering for the hundredth time what I should do. We had finished our meal and were drinking the last of the wine.

"Maybe I should go to London," I said uncertainly. "I'm so worried about her."

"Because of the phone call?"

"Yes—yes, I suppose mainly because of the phone call. If I thought she was merely busy carrying on with Cooper I would be reluctant to interfere, but I just can't believe that phone call has a completely innocuous explanation. I keep thinking about it."

"If you go to London," said Warren, "I'll come with you. If Gina's in any sort of trouble I want to be there helping her get out of it."

"Mmmm . . ." I was hesitant, not anxious to have him constantly at my elbow but willing to admit it would be pleasant not to face another foreign country alone. "Let me think it over. Can I call you later on this afternoon?"

"Sure." He found a pen and a scrap of paper and wrote down both his office and his apartment numbers. "I'll be home from work at six," he added, and then, glancing at his watch: "Talking of work I guess I'd better get back to the office. I've taken a long lunch hour."

Since he did not offer to pay for me we split the bill and then shook hands again as we parted in a stilted expression of comradeship. "Phone me as soon as you've made up your mind about London!" he called after me, as I made my escape. "I'll be all set to go, if necessary."

I seemed to be totally incapable of making up my mind on anything by that time. I could not decide whether I should go to London, and if I did go, whether I should go with Warren. I was afraid that after a few hours I would find him excessively annoying, but there are times when any companion is better than none at all, and this might easily be one of those occasions. On reaching the apartment again, I absent-mindedly made myself some coffee and sat down on the window seat to gaze out on the Parisian afternoon.

After some concentrated thought I came to the conclusion that the situation was less complex than anxiety made it appear. I would simply go to London. If I found Cooper I would look like a fool, but that was the worst that could happen; at least I would be on hand to help her. But if I stayed in Paris. . . . I shrugged. In that case I might as well have stayed in New York. The best thing I could do was to go to London, and if Warren was willing to help I should accept his offer. I might need all the help I could get. If he got on my nerves too badly I could always manage to escape from him.

I smiled wryly. Poor Warren! I really rather liked him. I finished my coffee and went to my handbag to find the paper with Warren's phone number on it. I was just looking at it a moment later when I had an idea.

Two minutes' searching around the living room produced the telephone directory, and sitting down on the floor, I opened it to the C section and began to turn the pages to Cooper. If he had an office in Paris which also served as a *pied-à-terre* for himself, it was possible it was listed under his name as well as under the name of the company.

It was. I saw the entry COOPER, GARTH, and the address in the Rue Piedmont, and on an impulse I reached for the phone and began to dial. It was logical to assume there would be a secretary there, or at least an answering service, and I could find out from them how long he was expected to be away from Paris and perhaps also the address of his office in London.

The number started to ring. I was just wondering in panic if the secretary or the answering service would speak English, when someone picked up the receiver.

A male voice said casually: "*Âllo?*"

I fumbled for the remnants of my school girl French vocabulary, but my mind, as so often happens in such a situation, went blank. "*Monsieur Cooper, s'il vous plaît,*" I said haltingly, and then added with an American accent which even I could hear: "*Est-il là?*"

There was a slight pause. Then:

"Yes, he's here," said the stranger in the perfect accentless English which only the British can produce. "You're speaking to him. May I ask who this is, please?"

4

I was so transfixed with embarrassment and surprise that I was dumbfounded. My fingers clasped the telephone receiver with a tight, hot, painful grip. My mind was blank, my tongue utterly paralyzed.

"Hello?" said Garth Cooper sharply. "Hello? Are you still there?"

I said very slowly: "Yes, I'm sorry. I wasn't aware that you were in Paris, Mr. Cooper. Please excuse me if I sound surprised." And remembering that he did not know who I was I added: "This is Gina's sister, Claire Sullivan."

Now it was his turn to be silent in astonishment. I tried to picture him, imagine his expression, but I could not.

"I've just arrived from New York for a vacation," I said, "but Gina doesn't seem to be here. I—I suppose you don't know where she is, by any chance?"

There was another slight pause. Then:

"She didn't know you were coming, did she?" he said unexpectedly. "She didn't mention it."

"No, it was a spur of the moment decision." I felt weak suddenly, dangerously close to tears. All my reassuring thoughts about Gina had sprung from the supposition that she was with Garth Cooper. To find out that he was back in Paris while she apparently was still in London was somehow horribly unnerving. "Mr. Cooper, if you know where she is—" I broke off, not knowing which words to choose.

"I last saw her in London," he said. "We flew over together last Friday evening, and on Saturday I introduced her to someone she wanted to meet, someone with show business connections. You know, no doubt, that she was hoping to break into films."

"Then you last saw her—"

"—on Saturday for lunch. I've been in Paris since Sunday night, but I'm returning to London again tomorrow morning. Perhaps I could make a few inquiries for you."

I did not know what to say. I was still so appalled by the realization that my worst fears had been proved valid that all I was conscious of was complete confusion.

"Perhaps we ought to discuss this in detail," said Garth Cooper after a moment. "Are you doing anything this evening?"

"No," I said numbly.

"Would you care to have dinner with me?"

"Well . . . if you're not too busy . . ."

"Not in the least," he said briskly. "Are you staying at Gina's flat?"

"Yes."

"Would it be convenient if I called for you at eight-thirty?"

"Yes . . . yes, it would. Thank you, Mr. Cooper."

"Not at all, Miss Sullivan," he said, very smooth, scrupulously courteous. " I look forward to meeting you."

And the line clicked with an air of finality as he replaced the receiver.

I had time on my hands, but did not know how to spend it. I should have passed the afternoon sight-seeing, visiting the Louvre perhaps, or Notre Dame, or Sacré-Coeur perched on the heights above Montmartre, but I had no heart for playing the rôle of tourist. I was too worried. For a while I considered canceling the date with Garth Cooper and going at once to London, but when I called the airlines I found that there were no seats available on the night flights across the Channel. On an impulse I made a reservation on the Air France morning flight, and then dithered for a while about whether or not I should contact my friend at Scotland Yard again. In the end I did put through a call to

Detective-Inspector Fowles, more to ease my mind than in any hope that the action would have startling results. But I was out of luck; he was away from the office. I left my name and phone number and wondered if I should have spoken to anyone else, but then decided that if I were to be in London tomorrow anyway I might as well spare myself making explanations to a stranger on the phone. Having settled that issue, I began to wonder if I might have been too ready to believe Garth Cooper when I had spoken to him earlier. It was not improbable that he had lied to me, and that he was after all connected with Gina's disappearance. I told myself I must guard against being too credulous when I met him that evening.

At length, unable to endure the confining walls of the apartment any longer, I went out and walked down to the river, but it began to rain and I was obliged to turn back again to the Rue St. Thomasine. Time passed; Candy-Anna returned from work and rushed out again at six-thirty on a date. Left alone once more I had a bath, changed slowly and by a quarter past eight was sitting on the window-seat and nervously watching the street below.

I began to wonder what he would look like. What, in general, did Englishmen look like? One had a stereotyped impression of Spaniards, Italians and Frenchmen being dark, slim and excitable, of Swedes, Danes and Norwegians being tall, blond and bland. Germans were fair and jolly with overweight tendencies, Slavs fair and sad with a fondness for melodrama. But the English? Would he be dark or fair? Fat or thin? Withdrawn or volatile? Perhaps, I thought, resorting to a familiar image, he would be like a typical New Englander, a reminder of the countryside where I had been born and brought up.

Logic rather than instinct told me this was unlikely. This man would be European, not American. He would think, act and speak like a European.

I was too inexperienced then to know that the English no more consider themselves part of Europe than they consider themselves part of America.

Below me in the street a taxi pulled up and my heart thudded in anticipation, but two very obvious Frenchmen got out and my nervousness receded. I glanced up and down the street. There was a woman, two children . . . and behind her a small man with middle European features. In the other direction walking up from the river were two more men, not together, of uncertain nationality. I was just wondering if either of these could be Garth Cooper when he came along.

To this day I have no idea why I should have been so positive of his identity as soon as I saw him, for he did not obviously stand out as a foreigner on French soil, but there was certainly no doubt in my mind. Perhaps the clue to his nationality was in his casual easy walk; Frenchmen are almost always either in a hurry or else idly stationary. His clothes were casual too, but not casual in the sense of being informal. On the contrary his suit was perfectly cut and his whole appearance immaculate, but he wore his clothes with an air of carelessness as if he knew he did not need to take trouble in order to look presentable. He had no hat, no umbrella and appeared to be unaware of the slight drizzle. Here was someone who expected it to rain a little during the course of each day and would have been surprised if it hadn't. His hands were in his pockets; as I watched, his right hand went to his head absentmindedly to smooth his hair, and then with a quick glance up and down the street he crossed over to the pavement beneath

44

my window and disappeared into the building.

I experienced a stab of nervousness followed by a wave of panic. I'm never very good at first meetings. With an abrupt, awkward series of movements I stood up, smoothed my dress over my hips, fidgeted with my collar and glanced in the mirror to check my appearance. I was just wishing I were four thousand miles away when the bell rang.

Moving very slowly I crossed the room and opened the door.

He smiled, polite, charming, unconcerned. "Miss Sullivan?"

"Mr. Cooper?" I said too efficiently, and opened the door a little wider. "Please come in."

"Thank you." He moved indolently across the threshold. His hair, which had looked dark at a distance, was in fact a light brown; I noticed again the trick he had of smoothing it with his hand as if he expected it to be perpetually untidy. He was tall, but not strikingly so, and without being solidly built he still managed to give an impression of durability. One felt he would wear well under adverse circumstances. He had a straight nose, a humorous mouth and wide set, unreadable light eyes.

"Can I offer you a drink?" I said uneasily.

"No, thanks," he said. "They have the most terrible bottle of whisky locked away in the bedroom somewhere, but since they always produce it with such enormous pride I haven't the heart to tell them it's undrinkable. Let's go straight out and have dinner. Incidentally, I must apologize for suggesting half past eight instead of half past seven. I forgot that Americans always eat early."

"When in Rome," I murmured, unable to think of anything else to say.

"Do as the Romans do?" he said. "Or do as your sister does and treat it like a little old-fashioned corner of Manhattan?"

I was unsure whether he was amused or not. "That's only a defense," I said. "One feels so foreign here."

"Depressing, isn't it?" he agreed, taking me aback. "The French look down their noses at anyone not born in France, but don't let it upset you. There's one race they hate even more than the Americans, and that's the British. They haven't yet got over Waterloo." He strolled over to the door again and held it open for me with a smile. "It'll be pleasant to dine out with a fellow-foreigner, for a change."

Since he had spent most of the previous week dining out with Gina I could not see why he should consider the prospect of dining with me a change but I made no attempt to argue with him. I opened my pocketbook, checked to see if I had my keys and glanced round the apartment automatically to see that all was in order. He waited by the doorway. The light from the corridor beyond seemed to slant oddly across his face, and as I passed him I looked up for no reason and found he was watching me with a closed, impassive expression which betrayed nothing.

I moved on, my face tingling, and felt his presence behind me as we moved down the corridor to the elevator. There was a curious, awkward silence. I was just racking my brains to think of some way of breaking it when he said lightly: "So this is what Gina would look like if she wasn't underweight and over-made-up!"

He meant it, I knew, to be a compliment, but I thought the remark disloyal and unfair to Gina.

"Gina's very attractive," I said glibly, not thinking.

"I didn't say she wasn't," he said in reply, and opened

46

the doors of the elevator as it reached our level of the shaft.

I really couldn't let the topic lapse on that dubious note so I said as we stepped into the elevator and he closed the doors after us: "I only wish I were as slim and as clever with my appearance as Gina is."

He pressed the button to the ground floor and the cage began to sink downwards. "Well, I shouldn't worry about it too much if I were you," he said. "You really don't need to."

I had taken him too seriously. My face began to tingle again and I turned aside to hide my embarrassment. Fortunately before any further conversation was necessary we reached the lobby and went outside into the wet street. He hailed a cab, and as I scrambled into the car I heard him say in perfect French to the driver: "*Le Cicéro, s'il vous plaît.*"

"Have you been to Paris before?" he asked neutrally, as the cab shot off over the cobbles.

"No," I said. "This is my first visit to Europe." A thought occurred to me. "Have you been to America?"

"I've been to New York," he said, "but I'm told that that's no more America than London is England."

"Did you like it?"

"Well, yes," he said frankly. "As a matter of fact, I did. One is supposed to shudder, I know, and say it was terrible, but I rather enjoyed it. I took a fancy to the Pan Am Building."

"That's near where I live!" I told him how I could see the building from the window of my apartment.

"You have one of those large modern apartments with every imaginable convenience?" he hazarded.

"Well, it's not considered modern," I said, "since it's at least ten years old, but I suppose it might seem large

47

to anyone who had previously lived in a cell. And the conveniences, though numerous, are imaginary, not imaginable. But it has a good view and it suits me and it's home, so I shouldn't complain."

He laughed. "It sounds like my apartment here in Paris!"

"But you have a bigger one in London?"

"Slightly bigger. But I don't like living in flats. My favorite place is a cottage I own in the country, in a village called Holmbury St. Mary in Surrey."

"You mean English villages really do have names like Holmbury St. Mary!"

He was amused. "That's a very modest example of a typical English village name! They come in much more exotic forms than that. My favorite name belongs to a village in the West Country called—if you can believe it—Compton Pauncefoot . . . hey, this driver's taking a very direct but unscenic route! We can do better than this." He leaned forward and began to speak in French. I caught the names *"Champs Elysées"* and *"Place de la Concorde"* and *"La Madeleine"*. The driver nodded wisely and turned the car into a sidestreet. "Since this is your first night out in Paris," said Garth Cooper, "you should be allowed at least a passing glance at a few landmarks."

And as he spoke the car swung into the Avenue Victor Hugo, and at the end of the wide boulevard I could see the floodlit splendor of L'Étoile and the Arc de Triomphe. Traffic roared past us, roared around us, roared behind us. Everyone seemed to be driving with a most reckless audacity. "Is traffic in Paris always like this?" I said doubtfully, remembering the stately pace of the New York avenues with the countless intervals of traffic lights and intersections.

"Always," came the wry reply.

We reached the Arc de Triomphe, circled it and hurtled into the Champs Elysées. There were lights among the trees, crowds strolling on the sidewalks and far away, at the end of the seemingly endless boulevard, more lights, a glimpse of greater brilliance to come.

I sighed.

"It's nice, isn't it?" said the man beside me. "I never get tired of it."

"Nice!" I said reproachfully, my eyes drinking in everything I could see and still thirsting for more. "What an understatement!"

"Where I come from everything is an understatement," he said. "It's good to hear someone who's not afraid to sound enthusiastic."

We traversed a smaller version of L'Etoile and went on down the Champs Elysées. There were buildings on either side of us now, enormous restaurant-cafés with tables on the pavement, hordes of people.

"Paris comes alive at night. When we come back this way later on there'll still be crowds everywhere."

"Is London like this too?"

"No, Londoners enjoy themselves secretively indoors in private clubs. Or else they cram themselves into a smoky little pub and see how much beer they can drink before closing time."

"*Are* the English really so odd?"

"We have to do something to preserve the illusion that we're different from any other race."

We reached the enormous width and breath of the Place de la Concorde; with a dexterity born of sublime confidence our taxi skipped nimbly in and out of other cars which were weaving diagonal and horizontal lines in front of us. We turned north to La Madeleine, then east

49

along the Rue St. Honoré and into the Rue de Rivoli which led past the Louvre.

"I'd like to go there and look around," I said wistfully, remembering that I was due to leave the following morning for London, and thought: I'll come back. As soon as I find out what's happened to Gina I'll come back here.

"You're interested in art, then?"

"In an amateur sort of way."

"Music?"

"Again—in an amateur sort of way."

"That means you must be highly professional at something!"

I laughed. "I teach English literature—I suppose you could say I was professional at that!"

"How interesting. Incidentally, what do the Americans really think of Shakespeare?"

" I suppose most of them are aware that he was born at Stratford-on-Avon, not Stratford, Connecticut."

"You surprise me. During August at Stratford-on-Avon one can almost imagine one is in Stratford, Connecticut. There's such a predominance of American accents in the High Street that I naturally assumed he was somewhat of a national figure in America."

I smiled. "The people who can afford to vacation in Stratford-on-Avon are usually people who have received a reasonable education."

"Do you like Shakespeare?"

"Yes—very much."

I thought he would make some comment at this point to reveal his own tastes, but he did not. Instead he leaned forward to say something else to the driver, and as he moved the glare from a street lamp momentarily threw a harsh light across his face and emphasized the fine line of his nose and jaw.

Somewhere far away, in the furthest recesses of my body, my heart skipped a beat and then went on as if nothing had happened.

He turned to face me again with his casual charming smile. "We're almost there. I hope you didn't mind the slight detour before dinner."

"On the contrary, I enjoyed it very much," I said. My mouth felt dry. My hands were clenched in tension and I consciously had to relax each finger. "Thank you." A mute voice was saying in my dulled brain: *not that. Please not that.*

Ever since I was old enough to distinguish between boys and girls, I seemed to have an unhappy knack of falling for men who were not only totally unsuitable but also totally uninterested in me. For a long time now I thought I had outgrown it, but now I began to wonder. It seemed as if my weakness had merely been in abeyance and was now showing unmistakable signs of awaking and returning to disrupt my life.

My hands clenched themselves again. I stared unseeingly out of the window as the car drew to a halt.

Outside the taxi I found myself in a narrow street leading off a wide boulevard, and presently we were making our way into a very plush, very intimate little restaurant where waiters fluttered like black and white moths and an imposing maître d'hôtel cruised across the thick carpet to greet us.

"Bonsoir, Monsieur Cooper, bonsoir, mademoiselle . . ." He bowed gracefully, flourished an elegant hand, summoned a minion to escort us to a secluded alcove. I forgot my fears of a moment ago; feeling immensely important and supremely élite I allowed the waiter to

51

pull out my chair and help to seat me as carefully as if my solid frame were as delicate as the most fragile china. A menu was put into my hands; I stared dizzily at all the French names and did not know where to begin.

"Do you want to try some French snails to start with?"

"I—don't quite feel brave enough for that," I said, overcome with cowardice. "After all, this is only my first evening in Paris. Is there something still French but not quite so exotic?"

"Vichyssoise?"

"Yes, that would be lovely."

We considered the menu for several minutes and made our decisions. A waiter took our order; Garth selected a wine. Finally when there was nothing more to do except to wait for our meal to be served, we sat back in our chairs and relaxed. Or at least, he did. I was too tense, too anxious to introduce the subject of Gina yet, not knowing how to begin, and in the end it was he who spoke first.

"I hope I'm not being too dense about this," he said casually, "but I'm still not really clear as to why you decided to come here on the spur of the moment without telling Gina. You don't strike me as being a scatter-brained little girl like Candy-Anna, so I find your actions all the more striking because they're so obviously out of character. Why did you decide to come?"

I hesitated for a moment, toyed with my snow-white napkin and smoothed it over my lap very carefully before I answered: "Your partner said nothing to you?"

"My partner?" he said astonished. "Lilian Jantzen? What does she have to do with your decision to come to Paris?"

"Gina called me from the Jantzens' apartment on

Saturday to urge me to come over." I decided against telling him the truth. "She sounded so carried away with Europe—so insistent that she was having such an extraordinary time—that my imagination was fired and I made this ridiculous spur of the moment decision. I knew Gina was planning to return to Paris by Monday so I thought I would surprise her by arriving Monday night—however, I did send a cable forewarning her so that my arrival wouldn't be too much of a shock. But when I got here I found she wasn't back from England and Candy-Anna had no idea where she was. That's why I called you this afternoon—I figured that as you'd been in London with her you might have some idea how I could get in touch with her."

"I'm afraid I know little more than you do." His eyes, steady, quizzical, interested, met mine. It was quite impossible to read his thoughts or guess if he were as honest as he seemed to be. "As I said to you on the phone this afternoon," he went on, "Gina was very eager to break into films—just as many successful young models are, I suppose. It so happens that my partner's husband, Eric Jantzen, who is an artist of some standing in London, has show business friends, and I thought there was a possibility that he might be able to provide Gina with some valuable contacts. I'd discussed the matter with him previously and he'd said that he'd be happy to meet her, so when we were both in London last Saturday I managed to introduce them to one another. I believe he invited her to his home for a drink that evening, so that would explain her presence in the Jantzen flat, even if it doesn't explain anything else. I can't see why on earth she put through a call to America from the flat of a more or less complete stranger. That simply doesn't make sense at all. What did she say?"

The arrival of the vichyssoise gave me time to consider my reply. "She had been trying to persuade me for some time to take my vacation in Europe," I said carefully, after the waiter had retreated. "I think her call was more of an impulsive, reckless gesture than anything else. A sort of gay, with-it, 'fun' gesture, if you can imagine what I mean. I know that sounds peculiar, but you knew Gina a little, didn't you?" I sipped my Vichyssoise, thankful of the opportunity to avoid looking at him as I spoke. "Gina is the sort of person who's quite capable of calling New York collect from the apartment of a stranger in London just to say 'why on earth don't you come over and join me?' It's just the sort of thing she would do."

He smiled. For some reason his smile made me feel uneasy, although I had no idea why it should. It was a friendly smile, frank, open and natural. There was nothing sinister about it at all, yet the sense of uneasiness persisted. "I don't actually know Gina very well, you know," he said after a moment. "In fact, although I met her about six weeks previously, I saw little of her until I returned to Paris from London about two weeks ago. Even then I only took her out a couple of times. She was having trouble with a difficult ex-fiancé."

"Yes," I said. "She wrote and told me that she had met Warren again in Paris."

"You know him? I thought he was a nice young chap, if a little stupid. If he had had an ounce of common sense he would have realized that the last way to win Gina was to chase after her like an infuriated terrier who enjoys a good bark. He met Gina by chance when I was with her, and although he joined us for a drink and the meeting began pleasantly enough, there was a rather unnecessary scene before he could be persuaded to retreat."

"It must have been embarrassing for you."

"Well, actually I was sorry for both of them—sorry for him because he was carefully destroying the impression he was trying to create in Gina's eyes, and sorry for Gina because I'm sorry for anyone with a difficult ex-fiancé. She was much more embarrassed than I was. I was really hardly involved—I didn't know her well enough for the scene to make any emotional impact on me."

I said lightly: "Candy-Anna spoke of you as if you were the big romance of Gina's life!"

"Candy-Anna reads too many romantic magazines." He spoke lightly too. His eyes were clear and unconcerned. "There had hardly been time for such melodrama."

Now I was certain that he was deviating a little from the truth. "She probably read some tremendous meaning into the fact that you and Gina traveled to London together," I said placidly. "She's just the sort of person who would fasten on something like that and exaggerate it out of all proportion."

He sipped his vichyssoise, effortlessly matching my attempt to appear nonchalant and unconcerned. "Probably."

I blushed, not knowing why, only feeling obscurely that his terse comment had been a rebuff. I made a great business of dabbing my mouth with my napkin and cast around in my mind feverishly for some way of changing the subject.

"Didn't the Jantzens mention to you that Gina had made the phone call from their apartment?" I said at last, remembering that my friend at Scotland Yard had contacted the Jantzens during his routine inquiry into the situation. "Didn't they mention it at all?"

"I haven't seen either of the Jantzens since early on Saturday," he said. "We all had lunch together with Gina. After that I was tied up for the remainder of the weekend on personal matters and then on Sunday night I returned to Paris."

"But haven't you spoken to them—to your partner—on the phone since then?"

"Yes," he said, "I spoke to Lilian this morning, but we never discuss by phone anything which isn't strictly business. Too expensive." He smiled. "We Europeans don't possess your American passion for the long distance call!"

"I hardly regard it as one of my ruling passions," I said dryly, remembering ruinous little bills arriving in the telephone company's discreet buff envelopes.

"Ah yes," he said, "I was forgetting. You have other, much more interesting ruling passions. How did you first become interested in Shakespeare?"

He was, I discovered during the course of the evening, extremely clever at manipulating the conversation into the precise channels which interested him. Throughout our long, elaborate and delicious meal I found myself talking far more than I normally did with a stranger; the wine was heady, powerful; my tongue seemed encouraged to give voice to a surprising amount of detail. I spoke of New England and New York, of a new life and a new world, of my parents, my work and my interests. We talked of the theatre, films, the written word, the spoken word, and I found myself to my amazement giving bold outspoken opinions in situations where reticence would normally have made me retreat or waver. Finally as we sat facing each other over the black coffee and Grand Marnier, I realized that he now knew a great deal about me whereas I still knew absolutely nothing about him.

"Which college did you go to?" I said, knowing that the English educational system was very different from the American but assuming he would have received some form of advanced education. "University, I mean, not college."

"I didn't go to a university," he said unperturbed. "My father went bankrupt so I was put out to work at an early age, like David Copperfield."

"Oh," I said, not knowing quite what to say. "But you graduated from high school—you obtained the usual diplomas?"

"By a fortunate chance I did, since my father thoughtfully staved off bankruptcy till I was seventeen, but it wouldn't have mattered if I'd been forced to leave school earlier. It was one of those schools where merely to attend it is supposed to open all doors later on, regardless of academic merit. Isay 'supposed to' because things are changing and now one is expected to learn something while attending school—a revolutionary idea, if ever there was one! My father would have been shocked."

"Is he dead?"

"Yes—perhaps fortunately for him. The world where he belonged died with the second world war. Afterwards in the late forties and early fifties there were too many changes for him." He spoke simply, with pity but without regret. "My mother died soon afterwards. I have a sister in New Zealand and three spinster aunts in Norfolk, but apart from them I'm as devoid of relations as you are. . . . I've never made up my mind whether that's a situation which calls for relief or regret. I suppose one is less restricted without relations, but—"

"—More lonely," I said. I was wondering how he had managed to make his money since he had clearly inherited nothing from his father. "When did you meet your partner? Have you known her a long time?"

"Yes, I met Lilian ten years ago when I was working in the china and glass department of a London store. I was a salesman and she was one of my best customers. One day, about six months after we first met, she asked me if I would like to try selling for her instead of for the department store. She was interested in the possibility of importing French china and glass and selling it in London—she knew people in the business, she'd worked in it herself, she thought she could create a market in certain glass which hadn't been imported since before the war. . . . Well, to cut a long story short, she had the money and the flair and she knew what she was doing. All I did was to sell a saleable product. Before we knew where we were, we found ourselves joint partners in a small but flourishing export-import business between England and France."

"I see." I could not quite believe he had ever been a mere salesman. He was so totally removed from my conventional picture of what a salesman should be like. "But do you—did you enjoy selling?"

"I enjoyed dealing with china and glass. Especially glass. Glass can be so beautiful, so exquisite. I always thought of selling as being nothing more than telling people who could afford to buy that they couldn't possibly spend their money in a more aesthetically pleasing manner. Do you know anything about glass?"

"Nothing at all."

He began to talk about it, interrupting himself only to order more coffee and liqueurs. Time, meaningless and unimportant, floated hazily away.

"Of course Lilian knows more than I do," he said at last after speaking with the authority and enthusiasm of an expert for some time. "She's taught me all I know." The phrase somehow struck a discordant note; he made an amused, impatient gesture with his hand as if to brush any possible *double-entendre* aside, and added frankly: "She's a remarkable woman."

"Yes," I said. "She must be. But what about her husband? Doesn't he have any part in the business at all?"

"Good God, no—Lilian wouldn't have that! Anyway, Eric's an artist, with a career of his own—the last thing he would want is to be involved in an office routine."

"I see."

"Of course, it was somewhat tricky when Lilian and I began our venture together. Eric was a little suspicious, I think, but he had no need at all to worry. I'm not interested, from the romantic point of view, in a woman ten years older than myself, and Lilian simply isn't interested in the romantic point of view. She's in love with her china and her glass."

I wondered why he felt it necessary to point this out to me; it was as if he were being automatically defensive on a subject which had caused him great difficulty in the past. I said impulsively, my mind veering back to Gina: "Do you think either of the Jantzens would know where Gina is? I'm really very worried about her."

He looked surprised. "Really? Why's that? I should think she enjoyed London so much over the weekend that she decided to stay on for a few days. After all she's a free lance model and can do as she pleases. And if Eric offered to introduce her to some show business contacts it's obvious she would stay on until she met them."

I nodded. Since I had misled him about Gina's

hysterical phone call to me, I could not expect him to understand my anxiety.

"Have you contacted the agency she works for? Maybe they've heard from her."

"Candy-Anna spoke to them today but they've heard nothing. In fact, they were very annoyed because she hadn't reported for work today. They had a special job lined up for her."

"Hm." He was silent. "I'll ask the Jantzens tomorrow if they know what's happened to her."

I nearly told him that I had resolved to go to London myself, but then held back at the last moment. It would be foolish to trust him too much. I had only his word that he had not seen Gina since Saturday afternoon, and I had already had the suspicion that he was minimizing the importance of his association with her. I felt depressed suddenly, tired; the glow of the wine had dulled and the sparkle of the evening seemed to have effervesced into nothingness. And then all at once his hand slid across the table to cover my own in a gesture I would never have expected from him, and his voice, concerned yet still casual, said quietly: "You really shouldn't worry, you know. I'm sure she's quite all right." I felt the tears blur my eyes and the sudden tightness hurt my throat because I knew that he was trying to be kind.

"Some more coffee?"

"No," I said, making an effort and overcoming my distress. "No, thank you. I feel completely satiated! It was the most wonderful meal and I enjoyed it very much."

"Would you like to go on somewhere else for a few more drinks?"

"No—no, really, I couldn't, thank you very much." The depression about Gina was enveloping me again and

60

I had a sudden absurd fear of bursting into tears in front of him and telling him more than I should about my predicament.

He glanced at his watch. "Well, the night's still young," he said lightly. "It's not even midnight yet. Would you like to drive into Montmartre and go up to Sacré-Coeur to see the city lights? Or would you like to stroll down the Champs Elysées for a little way? Or are you too tired and want to go back to the apartment?"

I nearly said: "Yes, perhaps if you'll excuse me . . ." but I did not. I looked up into his face and suddenly I forgot about my depression and my dread of losing my self-control. It didn't matter any more. Nothing mattered except that I was with him and that we were in Paris. I wanted to remember the evening as long as I lived and not mar a future memory by ending the evening too abruptly.

I said spontaneously: "Oh, I'd love to sit in one of those open sidewalk cafés on the Champs Elysées and watch the world go by!" and he laughed and said: "Why not? That's a splendid suggestion!" He paid the bill, leaving the notes carelessly on the check and not pausing to wait for change, and we left amidst the bows of the waiters and the good wishes of the Maître d'Hôtel. Outside it was warm and the night sky glowed in a reflection of a million lights and the cobbles of the street nibbled at my high-heeled shoes.

The next three hours are hazy in my memory, not because I was too tired to remember them but because they passed so quickly that afterwards my memory was only able to recall assorted moments. I can remember the smoke of Garth's cigarette curling upwards into the night air as we sat in the café on the Champs Elysées, the flame of the match reflected in his light eyes, the shadows his hands cast on the table. I can remember hearing the roar of the traffic yards away across the wide sidewalk, the murmur of the strolling passers-by, the incessant intensity of a strange language being spoken on all sides of me, but when I try to remember now I cannot hear our own voices or recall what we said. Later we took a cab to a place in Montmartre, danced a little, drank a little more, but I have no memory of being tired or even a clear recollection of the places we visited, until finally in the early hours of the morning we were on the steps of Sacré-Coeur and all Paris lay spread out before us beneath a summer moon.

"Oh!" I said, and the meaningless syllable expressed all that I felt at that moment, joy that the evening had exceeded my expectations, sadness that it was over and would almost certainly never be repeated, guilt that I could have forgotten Gina so completely when she had dominated my mind for so long. And as I sighed and went on gazing out over the city, he said casually from close at hand:

"How long do you intend to stay in Paris?"

The magic was broken. I don't know whether he was asking the question because he wanted to see me again or because he wanted to know what I planned to do next to find Gina. I moved a little, turning slightly away from him. "I don't know," I said. "My plans are uncertain."

After a moment he said: "What's the matter?"

"Nothing!" I was startled. "Why?"

"I thought perhaps something had disturbed you."

"No. I was only wishing that there could be more evenings as enjoyable as this one."

"I see no reason why there shouldn't be."

I did not answer.

"Unfortunately I can't cancel this trip to London tomorrow, or I'd most certainly do so. I'll be in London at least five days, possibly a week. If you were planning to go to England—"

"I have no plans at the moment," I said too abruptly, and moved back towards the white ghostly walls of Sacré-Coeur. "I'll have to think about that in the morning."

"Couldn't you think about it a little now?" I could hear his quiet footsteps behind me. "I'd like to see you again, and it seems pointless that we should have to spend the next week in different cities."

"Well," I said, trying to speak lightly and only succeeding in sounding hard and unnatural, "No doubt we'll both survive somehow."

I thought he would make some quick clever reply, but he was silent. Surprised by this unexpected reaction I turned to look at him. His face was still, his mouth shadowed, his light eyes as unreadable as ever.

"I'm sorry," I said wretchedly, knowing that he was upset even though there was no indication of it in his expression. "That was a stupid thing to say. Please forgive me."

He smiled at once, "It was no more than I deserved," he said pleasantly. "It was no business of mine to tell you how to spend your holiday. I'm the one who should apologize."

"No, I—"

"Ah, to hell with apologies and everything else!" he exclaimed in a sudden uncharacteristic burst of impatience, and the next moment without any warning at all I felt his arms slip around my waist and his lips, cool and hard, against my own. "And I'm sorry for that too," he said as he released me a second later, "if you think it

63

requires an apology. Since we're on the subject of apologies it seems appropriate that I should conduct all my apologizing at once. . . . Are you cold?"

" A little," I said, seizing on any excuse which would explain why the color had drained from my face and my body was trembling, "but not much."

"Let's go back into the square and find a taxi."

Twenty minutes later the cab was drawing up outside Gina's apartment house and Garth was telling the driver to wait. He escorted me to the front door, but when I started to thank him for the evening he took out his wallet and extracted a card.

"I enjoyed it as much as you did. Look here's my address and number—if you change your mind about coming to London call me as soon as you arrive and I'll come to meet you. And if you stay on in Paris, I'll call you as soon as I get the chance to fly back here from London."

The card felt smooth and cool beneath my hot fingers as I stared dizzily down at the address and phone number. I tried to say 'thank you' again, but I could not speak.

"Good night, then, Claire."

"Good night, Garth."

He kissed me again very briefly and was gone. I went into the building, shut the door, leaned against it. I heard the elevator arrive at the floor, the doors opening and closing around me, the ascent to my floor, and then I stood unmoving in the darkness of the apartment, as I recalled all that had been left unsaid between us. At last, after a long time, I reached out and switched on the light.

I saw the note almost at once. It was propped against the telephone and Candy-Anna had printed on it the words: CALL WARREN MAYNE WHEN YOU GET IN. URGENT.

I gave a small exclamation. Delving into my purse I found the right scrap of paper and began to dial the numbers with an uncertain, trembling hand.

"My God, Claire," said Warren plaintively. "It's nearly three o'clock in the morning! What's the big idea of calling up at this hour? I'm not a night owl."

I instantly felt guilty at my thoughtlessness. I had lost all track of time and had never even glanced at my watch. "I'm terribly sorry," I said, stricken. "But I've just got in and I saw Candy-Anna's note to say that I was to call at once as you had an urgent message—"

"For Pete's sake, doesn't that featherbrain ever get a message right? No, I've been calling you to find out whether you'd decided to go to England tomorrow. If you remember" he paused reproachfully "—you said you'd call me this afternoon at the office to let me know one way or the other."

"Oh, my goodness, I quite forgot!" I was stricken anew by my carelessness.

"Yes," said Warren politely. "Am I to take it that you've decided against going?"

"Well . . . no," I said confused. "I decided I would go. I've got a reservation on an Air France flight tomorrow morning. I—I'm so sorry, Warren—I should have let you know—"

He sighed. "I'll call Air France first thing tomorrow morning to see if they have a spare seat—what's your flight number? No, on second thought, it doesn't matter—I'll never be able to get the morning flight. I couldn't leave my office at such short notice. Tell you what I'll do—I'll try and get on an evening flight tomorrow. Which hotel did you plan on checking into?"

"I haven't the remotest idea," I said weakly, realizing

65

that Warren's companionship in London was now the last thing I wanted but not knowing how to deflect him from his inexorable course.

"Go to the Regent Palace. Or the Strand Palace. They're very good, very central, inexpensive and they cater to Americans, so you'll feel at home." And before I could even begin to explain to him that I would rather be in an English hotel among English people he added: "I'll try the Regent Palace first and if I find you haven't checked in there I'll try the Strand Palace. If you're not at either I'll meet you in the lobby of the Regent Palace at nine on Thursday morning."

"Yes," I agreed meekly, too exhausted to argue.

"Incidentally where the hell were you this evening? I called and called and finally at midnight I got hold of Candy-Anna. I was beginning to think you'd disappeared too. I was getting worried."

There was something vaguely touching about his earnest concern for me.

"I was just out seeing Paris," I said.

"Not alone!" He sounded shocked.

"Of course not," I said dryly. "Well, Warren, I apologize for not calling you back as we'd arranged—"

"But—" he interrupted and then remembered his manners. I could feel his curiosity permeating the wire which linked us, but he had neither the courage nor the effrontery to ask me outright who my escort had been.

"Yes?" I said mildly.

"Nothing. I'll see you tomorrow night, then. Okay?"

"Yes—many thanks, Warren."

"You're welcome," he said classically. "So long now, Claire."

" 'Bye."

I replaced the receiver with a sigh of relief and went

to bed as quickly as possible. My last thought before I slid into unconsciousness was to wonder what Warren would have said if he had known I had spent the evening with Garth Cooper.

My flight left at ten, but I saw him as soon as I entered the departure lounge. He was standing by the window and reading '*Le Figaro*'. The morning sun slanted across the fine bones of his face, and I saw that his expression was still and withdrawn with the effort of concentration. I stopped dead. I was just wondering why on earth it had never occurred to me that we would be on the same flight, when he looked up from the paper as if he knew he was being watched, and our eyes met. I saw him raise his eyebrows in quizzical astonishment, and as I blushed in confusion he smiled his easy charming smile, tossed his newspaper aside as if it no longer had any significance for him, and came casually across the room towards me.

5

"So you decided to come to London after all!" The last traces of his astonishment had merged into an expression of satisfaction. "I was hoping you'd come. When did you make up your mind?"

"Oh . . . not long ago," I said uncertainly, and felt myself begin to blush at the evasiveness of my answer.

"Did you have any trouble making your reservation?"

"No."

Fortunately at that moment our flight was called and his attention was diverted from me. We filtered out of the departure lounge, and five minutes later were seated in the plane and waiting for the moment when it would taxi away towards the runway for takeoff.

"You're a rather unpredictable person, aren't you?" murmured Garth mildly. "I thought you had quite decided to stay in Paris."

I smiled uncomfortably. "I had second thoughts."

"Really? Or had you planned to come to London all along?"

"I don't know why you should think that."

"It's not important." He smiled at me. "The point is that you're here. Do you like flying?"

"Sometimes I hate it a little less than others."

"This should be a good flight—we've got perfect weather for it."

I tried to look enthusiastic, but I suppose I was not very successful.

He laughed. "Wait and see!"

As it happened he was right and the flight was perfect, so perfect that I even forgot to feel nervous at the thought of so many thousands of feet of nothingness between me and the ground. We took off smoothly, soaring effortlessly away from Paris towards the west, and the sun shone with a dazzling brightness on the distant land below.

The stewardess was at Garth's elbow. "Something to drink, monsieur?"

"Yes," said Garth, and to me: "This should be a celebration to mark your first visit to England. How about some champagne?"

"Oh!" I said, flabbergasted at the idea of champagne

before noon, and thought fleetingly how shocked my parents would have been at anything like this. "Well, it would be nice," I said guiltily. "Delightful, in fact."

Garth turned to the stewardess. "Champagne for two, please."

The plane soared on, and suddenly I could look out of the window and see the coast, the flicker of white as the waves broke against the rugged cliffs of the French coast far below. I was just giving an exclamation of pleasure when the champagne arrived.

"Drink up," said Garth. "We're nearly there."

"But we haven't even crossed the Channel yet!"

"That'll only take five minutes."

It seemed to take even less than that. We had no sooner left the French coast behind when I saw the coast of England approaching.

"Where are the White Cliffs?"

"We're further north than that, I think."

We left the Channel behind. There was a river below us, an enormous estuary. Little patchwork squares of fields surrounded each of the towns we passed, until gradually the area became densely populated and I guessed we were approaching London.

"You see that winding river over there?"

I nodded. "Is that—"

"The Thames. It looks as if we're going to fly over central London."

And then came the most perfect part of all. The plane took a westward course parallel to the line of the river and I saw Tower Bridge, the Tower of London, the dome of St. Paul's, the spires of a thousand churches, the Houses of Parliament, Westminster Abbey. . . .

"Exactly like the photographs," I said amazed, as if I had always secretly suspected the camera of lying.

There seemed to be an endless number of bridges over the river, some plain solid structures, some elaborately gothic and fanciful. I gazed down at them all with fascination and hardly even noticed the plane losing height as we flew on over the west London suburbs towards the airport. When our wheels touched the ground ten minutes later I was conscious, for the first time after a flight, of regret that the journey was over.

"That was wonderful!" I said frankly to Garth as we unfastened our safety belts. "If all flights were like that I'd look forward to them more often. And thank you so much for the champagne."

We had the usual tedious wait at Customs and Immigration, except that he, with his British passport, was processed through the official machine more quickly than I was.

"Where do I get a bus to the terminal?" I asked, confused by the airport mêlée and looking around for an information sign.

"You don't want to bother with a bus," said Garth. "I never do. We'll take a taxi. Incidentally, where were you planning to stay?"

"Warren Mayne suggested the Regent Palace. Or the Strand Palace. Do you know them?"

"Yes," he said non-committally. "They're both very central. The Regent Palace is just off Piccadilly Circus."

"That sounds fine."

We found a cab and set off east again. The road was wide and modern, the countryside around the airport extraordinarily green and lush to my eyes, but presently the countryside ended and the suburbs began. As we approached the city there were more towering modern buildings and a massive elevated road which reminded me of the Pulaski Skyway outside New York City.

70

"It's not how I imagined London to be," I said doubtfully. "Everything's so modern."

"Did you expect the roads to be full of horse-drawn carriages?"

I laughed, glanced around me at the traffic. "So many tiny cars," I said, "and all driving along on the wrong side of the road. There are hardly any big cars at all."

"There's no room for them."

We drew nearer to Central London. There was a wide main street called Cromwell Road bordered with trees and stately houses.

"Are those houses old?"

"No, fairly new. I don't suppose any of them are more than a hundred years old."

London flashed on past the windows of the taxi. Garth was mentioning English names to me, names familiar yet strange. "This is Kensington . . . Knightsbridge. . . . The park on the left is Hyde Park . . . this is Hyde Park Corner . . . Piccadilly . . . Green Park on the right. . . ."

"So many parks," I said astonished. "And how gracious the houses are here."

We reached the tiny Piccadilly Circus and almost at the same time the Hotel Regent Palace. Garth helped the driver with my luggage.

"How about dinner this evening? I can call for you at about six-thirty and we can go somewhere for a drink first . . . and I'll talk to the Jantzens about Gina. All right?"

"Yes . . . thank you. . . ." I was dazed, overcome by the strangeness of the new country.

"You have my office number if you should want to contact me, haven't you? Till tonight, then." He touched my shoulder lightly but did not kiss me. "Au revoir."

"Goodbye—and thank you."

71

He got into the cab again. I heard him say abruptly to the driver: "Sixty-two Half Moon Street," and he turned and raised his hand briefly to me as the car drew away from the pavement.

I stood watching the car turn towards Piccadilly Circus, and then, still feeling dazed, I left the street and went very slowly into the hotel.

Fortunately they had a room available on the fifth floor, and after I had unpacked my luggage and redone my makeup I sat down on the bed and placed a call to the apartment in Paris. I had the nagging suspicion that as soon as I had left Paris Gina had returned to it, but my suspicions proved groundless, for no one answered the phone. Candy-Anna was evidently out working and there was no one else there. Having satisfied myself that Gina was still missing I wondered whether to call Scotland Yard again. I remembered that I had phoned from Paris and asked my friend to call me back, but he had probably returned the call while I had been out with Garth the previous evening. I hesitated. Perhaps I should wait till Garth had talked to the Jantzens. I had little enough information to give to Scotland Yard at present, beyond the fact that she had not after all been with Garth when she had phoned me the previous Saturday. But whose word did I have for that? Only Garth's. If I called Scotland Yard again they would begin questioning Garth, prying into his movements. . . .

I would wait, I thought: I would wait until he had talked to the Jantzens. I instinctively shied away from making a move which would involve him in considerable embarrassment and perhaps estrange him from me. Besides, I believed him. I was quite convinced that he was speaking the truth.

Or was I?

I went restlessly over to the window and stared out over Soho. I was still thinking of Garth a moment later when the phone rang and I went back to the bedside to answer it.

"Miss Claire Sullivan?" said the operator in the building. "One moment, please. I have a call from Paris."

For one long moment my heart thudded in relief, and then the next instant I was listening not to Gina, as I had hoped, but to Warren Mayne.

"Claire? Hi, I thought I'd just call and find out if you arrived safely and managed to check in all right. How was the flight?"

"Fine, thanks." It was thoughtful of him to have phoned and I tried to sound cheerful. "I enjoyed it."

"Good. Look, I managed to get a seat on the flight leaving at six this evening so I should be with you around eight-thirty or so."

"I—"

"I checked with the reservation people at your hotel and they have a room for me for tonight. I'll give you a call when I get in."

"Yes, but—"

"Hey, I'll tell you something odd. I called up Garth Cooper's Paris office this morning to find out when he was expected back in Paris, and they told me he'd just left for London! So he was in Paris yesterday and possibly the day before as well."

"Yes."

"You mean you knew?"

"He was on my flight this morning."

"He was?" He sounded blank with astonishment.

"Yes, we traveled over together. He—"

"But how did you know him?"

73

"What?"

"How did you know him from Adam? How did you get talking to one another?"

"Oh . . . I met him last night, as it happens. I called him to ask about Gina and he stopped by at the apartment."

"He did?" Warren was frankly incredulous. "Why didn't you tell me, for God's sake?"

"When I last spoke to you it was three o'clock in the morning and you weren't in a receptive mood for a long story. Besides, there was no news. Garth said he hadn't seen Gina since lunch on Saturday."

Warren sounded as if he was just about to voice a very rude word indeed, but fortunately he stopped in mid-syllable.

"It might be true," I said impassively. "I'm having dinner with him tonight so I hope to find out more details from him then."

"You're having dinner?" Warren said, amazed. "With him? Tonight?"

"Yes, so I won't be in when you arrive. If I find out anything I'll call your room as soon as I get in."

"But—" He was speechless. Then: "Do you think that's wise? Hell, I don't want you disappearing too! Can't you change it to drinks at nine? Then I'll be able to join you and see that you're all right—"

I was beginning to believe Warren had been born in the wrong century. He should have been a knight rescuing damsels in distress.

"Please don't worry," I said politely. "I'm quite capable of looking after myself and I don't really believe Mr. Cooper is involved in the white slave traffic. I'll talk to you tonight, Warren—I hope you have a good flight. Thanks for calling."

I managed to get rid of him without sounding too rude, but I sensed that his faith in my level-headedness had suffered a mortal blow. I paused for a moment and felt my own faith waver. Was it possible that sanity had temporarily deserted me and that I had made an appalling mistake by trusting Garth? A shiver edged its way down my spine suddenly. Fumbling in my bag I drew out his card, picked up the receiver and asked the operator to try his office number for me.

I could hear the bell ringing at the other end of the wire. Then: "Cooper-Jantzen—good afternoon," said a girl's voice. "May I help you?"

"Good afternoon," I said. "Could you tell me the nature of your firm's business, please? I'm conducting a survey for purposes of market research."

"We deal in the importing and exporting of china and glass between England and France."

"I see. Thank you."

"Do you wish to speak to Mrs. Jantzen?"

"No, thank you. Is Mr. Cooper there?"

"No, I'm afraid Mr. Cooper's out of the country at present."

"Oh . . . I see. Thank you. Goodbye." I replaced the receiver slowly. Garth had told me the previous evening that urgent business in London prevented him from staying on in Paris, but apparently the business had not been urgent enough to necessitate him calling his office. I wished with annoyance that I had asked the girl when she expected him to return to London, and then wondered if there had been any reason on his part to return without telling his partner. Perhaps, after all, he was not as honest as I had supposed him to be.

Uneasiness, faint and nebulous, shadowed my mind for a moment. I pushed it aside, determined not to let my imagination lead me astray, and, seizing my handbag, I went briskly downstairs and stepped out of the hotel to explore Piccadilly.

I did not walk far since all the strain and exhaustion of the last few days seemed to choose that afternoon to catch up with me, and when I returned to the hotel I spent the remainder of the afternoon resting. At five I got up, bathed and changed; at six-thirty I was just putting the finishing touches to my appearance when the house phone rang. It was Garth, in the lobby. My heart began to beat a fraction quicker. With my mouth dry and my hands unsteady, I left the room a second later and went downstairs to meet him.

"How nice you look!" he said as he came forward towards me. "Not in the least tired. No one would ever have thought you'd spent the morning drinking champagne thirty thousand feet above the English Channel. Did you do anything special this afternoon?"

"No, I just spent the time recovering from the champagne above the Channel! What about you? Did you go to your office?"

"Actually, I didn't let Lilian know I was back until five o'clock this afternoon. I have to admit I wanted some sleep as much as you did so I went straight to my flat. Incidentally, talking of Lilian, I thought you might be interested in meeting both the Jantzens, so I've invited them to have drinks with us at my club before dinner. I hope that's all right with you?"

"Yes—yes, of course. I'd like to meet them. Did you ask Mrs. Jantzen about Gina when you spoke to her?"

"Yes." He opened the door for me and we walked out into the street. Then: "Why didn't you tell me you'd phoned Scotland Yard to investigate Gina's call?"

I caught my breath. I felt my cheeks slowly begin to

76

burn as I wondered how I could have been so stupid not to have foreseen this happening.

"Lilian said they'd had a man around from the Yard as the result of Gina's phone call to you. I presume it was you who suggested that the Yard should investigate."

"Yes," I said reluctantly, too embarrassed to look at him. "It was me."

A cab drew up beside us in response to his raised arm, and as we got inside Garth gave the driver the name of his club.

"What made you think it was a matter for Scotland Yard?" Garth asked pleasantly, as we drove into the vortex of Piccadilly Circus and crowded our way through the traffic around Eros. "What made you get in touch with them?"

After a while I said: "I was worried."

"I should imagine you were," said Garth with amused irony, "if you troubled to phone Scotland Yard from New York."

I was unable to reply.

"What exactly did Gina say during the call?" he said presently. "There must have been rather more to the conversation than you implied."

"It was just that we were cut off," I said in a rush. "And when I traced the call and phoned back there was no reply. I suppose I panicked."

He looked at me oddly as if he suspected I was still keeping part of the truth from him, but made no comment.

"What did the Jantzens say?" I said clumsily, stammering a little. "Did they know anything that would explain the situation?"

"Not really. Lilian was the one who let Gina into the flat but then she had to dash out to meet some friends so she wasn't with her for more than a few minutes. Eric, whom Gina wanted to talk to about show business contacts, was delayed and apparently when he got home Gina had gone. He assumed she hadn't bothered to wait for him and thought no more of it till the police turned up later to investigate. Before they arrived he tried phoning her hotel to apologize for letting her down, but was told she had left that evening."

"Before or after she had been at the Jantzen apartment?" I asked quickly.

"I don't think he bothered to establish that. He called the hotel before the police arrived—before he knew anything was wrong. At that stage he didn't even know Lilian had let Gina into the apartment. When the police told him she must have been there he assumed for some reason that I had let Gina in, although why he should have thought that I would be with her I can't imagine. *I* wasn't interested in hearing about his show business contacts."

"But you have a key to the Jantzen apartment?"

"Yes, I stayed there once and had a key made. I still use it occasionally to entertain clients. We always do, since it's much more spacious than mine. For that matter, Lilian has a key to my cottage in Surrey as well, since very occasionally we have clients up for a weekend in the country."

But I was thinking of Gina again. "Which hotel was she staying at?"

"The Westbury, off Bond Street."

"Then if we could prove she checked out from there after making her phone call to me it would prove that at least she was safe after leaving the Jantzen apartment!"

"I'm sure she's safe anyway," said Garth frankly. "To be honest I think she's gone chasing off after one of the contacts Eric mentioned at lunch on Saturday. When he

78

appeared to forget about her on Saturday night I expect she lost patience with him and decided not to wait around any longer. It would be just like Gina to race off impulsively with the idea that she could conquer show business single-handed."

"I thought," I said, "you didn't know Gina very well."

He smiled slightly. "You don't trust me, do you?" He glanced out of the window. "This is Pall Mall," he said absently. "At the end here is St. James's Palace. Then we swing up St. James's Street into Piccadilly again."

I stared out of the window with unseeing eyes.

"You think something happened to her in the Jantzen flat?" he asked quite suddenly.

I nodded, not looking at him.

"Did she sound frightened?"

"Yes."

"Did she scream? Gasp? Call out?"

"No . . . no, she just hung up in the middle of the call without a word of warning."

"That's odd . . . It seems to me that if, for example, a burglar had entered the flat and accosted her she would have screamed when he arrived on the scene. But if she hung up of her own accord the burglar explanation seems unlikely."

"Yes," I said unsteadily. "I guess so."

"Actually there's not much that could have happened to her. Why should the Jantzens wish her any harm? They barely knew her. There was no reason why she should have been frightened of them."

"No . . ."

"Presumably the police will already have established what time she left the Westbury, so we can get in touch with them this evening, if you like, to find out the exact details and to report that she's still missing."

"And if she checked out after she made the phone call and not before—"

"We'll know nothing happened to her at the Jantzen flat." He hesitated slightly. "You're sure," he said, "you're quite sure she hadn't had too much to drink? I hardly like to ask such a question but it's the only simple explanation I can think of."

"No, I'm sure she hadn't," I said at once. "And if that was all that was wrong, she'd be back in Paris by now."

"That's true."

We turned off Piccadilly into a complicated network of short streets.

"This is Mayfair," said Garth as we passed rows of elegant houses and a few exclusive-looking shops. "We're almost at my club."

The taxi made a right turn and drew up outside a stately townhouse with marble pillars flanking the front door.

"Here we are." He got out first and helped me to the pavement beside him before he paid the driver. As the cab drove off again we went into the house and moved through a series of lobbies, past a magnificent staircase with wrought iron banisters, and eventually into a small intimate bar which faced onto a patio.

"They don't seem to be here yet," said Garth, glancing around at the occupants of the room. "Shall we sit outside or will it be too cool for you?"

"No, I'd prefer to be outside."

He escorted me to a table shaded with a multicolored umbrella and as we sat down a waiter came over to take our order.

"A Tom Collins?" I said doubtfully.

The waiter gave a supercilious smile.

"Try a gin and tonic," said Garth, and as I acquiesced

gratefully he added to the waiter: "And a dry martini, please."

As the waiter disappeared into the bar a man and a woman passed him on their way out to the patio. Garth saw them a second after I did, and raised his hand in greeting.

"We couldn't find you!" the woman called. "What are you doing hiding under that ridiculous umbrella?"

"Didn't you read in the paper that it's been the hottest July afternoon for thirty years?"

They laughed, and as they came over towards us I was conscious of a stab of surprise, for they were not as I had expected them to be. I think I had anticipated a sophisticated, polished couple, the wife glamorously efficient, the husband glamorously artistic. But there was little glamor. Lilian Jantzen was plump and blonde and plainly but not outstandingly well dressed; she wore a navy blue linen suit with conventional but unflattering white accessories. She reminded me of a housewife who, having received an unexpected invitation out, snatched the first available outfit from her wardrobe and dressed absentmindedly while planning the next day's shopping list. The result was passable but lacking in impact. Eric Jantzen was also fair and plump, and had a jovial smile which instantly reminded me of the more obvious breed of American salesman. I reflected with amusement how ironic it was that Garth, who at least looked as if he *could* have artistic talent, was the salesman while Jantzen, who looked like a salesman, was in fact the artist.

Garth introduced us. There was much smiling and shaking hands and then we all sat down again. The waiter returned with our drinks and took the Jantzens' order; I noticed that it was Lilian Jantzen, not Eric, who did the ordering, and that she ordered without consulting her husband.

"How nice," said Lilian absently, glancing around the patio. "This place has improved, Garth." She began to peel off her gloves. "Well, welcome to England, Miss Sullivan! I'm sorry to hear that you've had all this worry about your sister."

"We were both sorry," said her husband. He made it sound like a correction. "Both of us. We don't understand what could have happened. We thought—"

"Have you spoken to Scotland Yard again?" said Lilian to me without waiting for him to finish. "Have they any more news?"

"No," I said. "I thought I would check with them later."

"I'm quite sure nothing serious can have happened to her," she said reassuringly. "She struck me as being a very capable sort of girl who knew exactly where she was going."

"Yes," I said doubtfully, not certain whether I could recognize Gina from this description. "I mean, do you think so?"

"Oh yes!" She was placid, confident. She smiled at me warmly and her eyes lost their vague, abstracted expression, as if she were perpetually thinking of something else more important, and mellowed to a softer, kinder shade of blue. It occurred to me that twenty years ago she would have been a pretty woman. "Gina was alert—intelligent—ambitious. How can one be a successful model otherwise? I personally think she must have flown off to Rome to meet Dino di Lasci, that film producer Eric knows. Eric mentioned him to her at lunch last Saturday and Gina probably got it into her head then and there to go to Rome as soon as possible."

"Then why did she go to your apartment at all on Saturday evening?" I said hesitantly. "If there was no need for her to go—"

"Eric was going to discuss the situation with her in detail, but unfortunately he got delayed and I suppose she lost patience and left. She would still have been in time to catch the night flight to Rome, I should imagine."

Garth said, toying idly with the stem of his glass: "But why the long distance phone call, Lilian? Why call America?"

Eric Jantzen shrugged. "She was young and excited— why not?" I noticed for the first time that he spoke with a faint foreign accent which I could not identify. "She wanted her sister to come to Europe to share in the good times she was having."

"My dear Eric," said Garth, "Claire didn't call in Scotland Yard because Gina was bubbling over with *joie de vivre*."

Jantzen succeeded in looking perplexed. His round, rather comical face puckered between the eyebrows. "Perhaps a burglar tried to break and enter—she became frightened—"

"A burglar?" Garth interrupted. "Don't you mean a kidnapper? It seems that the only item which is missing since the phone call is Gina herself."

"You're full of destructive criticism, Garth," said Lilian lightly, but she did not sound annoyed. She looked at him with those mild warm blue eyes and smiled a mild warm smile, but he did not see her. He was still fingering the stem of his glass and watching the liquid nudge the sliver of lemon peel towards the rim.

"Cigarette, Miss Sullivan?" said Eric Jantzen to me suddenly.

"I don't smoke, thank you."

"Lilian?"

"No, thank you, dear." She gave an identical smile but spoke more absent-mindedly as if to reproach him for distracting her. She glanced back at Garth: "Have you any constructive suggestions instead of destructive criticisms?"

"None that I can really believe in." He accepted a cigarette from Eric Jantzen and fumbled in his pocket for a light.

"Ah, that's just it!" said Jantzen, laughing jovially as if Garth had made a witty remark. "One resorts to the preposterous—visitors from space, perhaps. Or ghosts. Or—"

"Please, dear." Lilian's voice was so extraordinarily placid that I had to look at her to see how annoyed she was. "It's hardly a joking matter."

Jantzen subsided like a pricked balloon.

The waiter chose that moment to arrive with their drinks and presently we had drunk a perfunctory toast and were sipping sociably at our glasses.

"She didn't give you any hint of what she might be planning, I suppose, Garth?" said Eric Jantzen presently as if eager to prove he could discuss the situation with complete seriousness. "She didn't confide in you?"

Lilian was unimpressed. She was just turning to me and opening her mouth to make some remark when Garth said: "Should she have done?"

"I thought you and she were—" He stopped, glanced sunnily around the table and then began to look dismayed as he realized the observation was going to be hard to finish. "She seemed to—admire you?" he suggested tentatively. "Hadn't you been seeing her in Paris? I thought—"

"Really, dear," said Lilian. "there's no need to make

84

Bohemian observations to remind us you're an artist." She stifled a yawn. "It was perfectly obvious that Gina was in love with her career, not Garth."

Jantzen's silence was a more eloquent denial than any words would have been. There was a pause. Then:

"I rather agree with you, Lilian," said Garth idly, "but I suppose we did get on well together on the few occasions when we met. She was bright and amusing and entertaining in her own way." His eyes met mine across the table; the wink he gave me was so quick that afterwards I almost wondered if I had imagined it. "But I prefer a different kind of entertainment."

The muted loudspeaker system which the club used for announcements murmured in the rooms around us and we all started slightly as we heard Garth's name.

"Telephone call for Mr. Garth Cooper . . . Mr. Garth Cooper . . . telephone."

Lilian shed her abstractedness as if it were a redundant article of clothing and was instantly on the alert. "A business call, do you suppose? But no one knows you're back!"

"I phoned Briggs and Douglas from my flat this afternoon over the Rémy contract. Excuse me, please, everyone." He stood up and disappeared quickly indoors just as I remembered that he had told me earlier how he had spent the afternoon sleeping and had not even phoned Lilian until five to announce his arrival.

The Jantzens were looking at one another. Presently Eric Jantzen said speculatively: "Thérèse, perhaps?"

"Probably."

They were silent. About five seconds drifted away, floating upwards into nothingness with the steadiness of the smoke from Eric's cigarette. Then:

"Who is Thérèse?" I said hesitantly at last.

"Thérèse?" said Lilian, vaguely surprised. "He didn't tell you? She is—was—his fiancée. Such a tiresome woman! I was so glad when he finally extricated himself from the engagement a month ago."

6

For a moment I forgot my surroundings, forgot the patio with the gay umbrellas, forgot the Jantzens who were so pleasantly relaxed yet so subtly on edge with each other. I was back in Paris again, talking to Garth of Warren and Gina, and Garth was saying: "I always feel sorry for anyone with a difficult ex-fiancé." Possibilities and answers began to flash confusingly through my mind; if Gina had somehow met Thérèse, if Thérèse had thrown a scene or threatened trouble, it was conceivable that Gina might have become distraught and run away. I said quickly, not even waiting to allow the ideas to crystalize into theories in my mind: "If they're no longer engaged then why is Thérèse calling him? Are they still on friendly terms?"

"My dear," said Lilian in a voice fraught with implications, "friendly is hardly the word to describe the curious attitude Thérèse had towards Garth. She still hasn't accepted the broken engagement and simply refuses to be reasonable—or even dignified—about the situation. She seems to think that by storming around creating passionate scenes and being fanatically jealous, he'll finally give in and agree to go through with the wedding." She made a neat, fastidious gesture of distaste. "So unnecessary! But then what can you expect of the French? With them nothing is ordinary or restrained; everything is *La Grande Passion*."

"Does she live in Paris?"

"No, she lives in London and works for the French Embassy. I must say, I'm disappointed in her behavior—even the French could surely be expected to be more sensible about a broken love affair! Goodness me, it happens every day!"

Eric Jantzen said to his scotch on the rocks: "She was *in love* with the man."

"Heavens, dear, I hardly think *love* gives one the excuse to act in such an uncivilized manner!" She spoke with a detached incredulity as if love were a trival illness to be dispelled by two aspirin and a ten-minute nap. "No, I was disappointed in Thérèse. She was a mature, attractive woman—very soignée. In some ways she would have been exactly right for Garth, although, mark you, I suspected from the beginning that she would be too possessive to tolerate the little light-headed flirtations he indulges in from time to time—"

There was a chill in the air suddenly. I felt cold, desolate.

"When one's engaged," said Eric Jantzen, "one is expected to flirt with one's fiancée, not with other women."

"Good gracious, dear, you talk as if Garth were an absolute Casanova! You know as well as I do that he's equally charming to every woman he meets—why, I'm certain Miss Sullivan will bear me out on that!—but he seldom really *intends* to be flirtatious. It's the women who read flirtatiousness into his attentions! And since Thérèse is pathologically jealous she would be bound to consider every small attention as a sign that he was conducting, or trying to conduct, an illicit affair."

"I don't suppose Thérèse was any more jealous than another woman would have been in the same circumstances."

"I disagree," said Lilian shortly. "She was totally unreasonable. It was a good thing they called off the engagement. If they'd married I'm sure Garth would have found her quite impossible to live with."

Eric Jantzen was eloquently silent again. Driven by a compulsion to shatter that silence, I said hurriedly: "Did Gina meet Thérèse?"

The question seemed to surprise them; they both looked at me sharply before looking at one another.

"She didn't mention it," said Lilian doubtfully. "I wouldn't have thought it was very likely. No, she couldn't have. If Thérèse met Gina with Garth there would have been a big scene and Garth would have mentioned it to us later. But he said nothing."

"I—I was thinking that if there had been some sort of scene—in your apartment—if Thérèse had found Gina there with Garth—"

"But why should Thérèse go to our apartment?" said Eric Jantzen, brow puckered again. "There was no reason why she should."

"She might have followed Garth there," said Lilian. "Garth might have arrived after I left Gina alone in the flat."

"But Garth said he wasn't there!"

"Perhaps there *was* a scene and he didn't mention it." She looked thoughtfully at her glass of sherry. "Perhaps there was an unpleasant scene, so unpleasant that he had to take Thérèse away. Then Gina, who was distraught and shocked, made the phone call. And replaced the receiver when Garth returned." She looked across at me, ignoring her husband. "Do you think that makes sense?"

"It makes better sense than any other theory I've heard so far," I said hesitantly. "But why didn't Garth mention any of this to us? And why didn't Gina call me back later to explain what had happened? And where's Gina now?"

Lilian shrugged. "Perhaps we're wrong." She glanced towards the French windows which led from the bar to the patio. "Here he comes . . . Garth, did Gina meet Thérèse last weekend?"

Garth stopped so abruptly that he might have been jerked to a halt by an unseen hand. His face became closed, remote, his expression betraying nothing.

"Do we have to talk about Thérèse, Lilian?" It was the first time I had ever heard him angry. "Is it really necessary?"

"No, dear," said Lilian vaguely in exactly the same tone of voice as she used to her husband. "Not really. I was merely being rude and inquisitive. Was that Douglas on the phone about the Rémy contract? What did he say?"

"No, it wasn't Douglas. It was a personal call from a friend of mine." He sat down quickly at the table and took several swallows of his drink before glancing at his watch. "We must be going, Claire. It's later than I thought it was."

"Oh Garth!" said Lilian, half reproachful, half annoyed. "After only one drink? I haven't even had the chance to ask Miss Sullivan about herself yet!" She smiled at me encouragingly. "You'd like another drink, wouldn't you, Miss Sullivan?"

"Well, as it happens . . ." I searched for an excuse and then decided to tell the truth. "I've had a lot to drink already today, and I'm not really accustomed to liquor, perhaps I'll just settle for one drink this time. But don't please let me stop you from having another—"

"Maybe some other time, Lilian," said Garth. "Perhaps we can all have dinner together before Claire leaves London. Meanwhile I'm afraid you'll have to excuse us."

Lilian sighed resignedly and made a gesture of disappointment with her plump, neatly manicured hands. "As you wish."

We finished our drinks and went back indoors and through the house to the lobby.

"Well, I'm glad we had a chance to meet, Miss Sullivan," said Eric Jantzen pleasantly as we parted. "Sorry it was so brief. You must be sure and see us again before you leave."

"Thank you—yes, I should like to," I replied.

Lilian said: "How long do you intend to stay?"

"I—I'm not sure. Another few days, perhaps."

"Well, I do hope you have good news soon about your sister." She took my hand in hers and squeezed it sympathetically. "Garth, you'll let us know, won't you, if there's any news? I really felt quite concerned, especially as she apparently chose our flat to disappear from. However, I'm sure nothing serious can have happened. Perhaps Eric's right after all, and she flew off to Rome to see di Lasci." But she sounded doubtful, as if Eric was so seldom right that this possibility was most unlikely.

The doorman flagged two cabs; Garth and I got into the first, and, looking back over my shoulder, I saw the Jantzens about to get into the second. Eric Jantzen paused to wave a brief farewell in our direction.

"He seems pleasant enough," I said, raising my hand automatically in response. "But doesn't Lilian give him rather a hard time?"

"They've always been like that, ever since I've known

them," said Garth. "I suppose they're both used to it by now." He turned to face me, and his nearness suddenly seemed overwhelming. "I'm sorry," he said, "for rushing you away like that. It was simply that—" He stopped.

There was a silence.

"Yes?" I said nervously.

His light eyes were hard and angry. "I wanted to be alone with you," he said abruptly. "I wanted you to hear about Thérèse from me, not from the Jantzens."

After a moment I said, "Lilian didn't mean to be indiscreet. She was just wondering if—"

"If Gina and Thérèse had ever met. I didn't answer her question, did I? Well, I'll answer it now. Yes, they did meet. They met last weekend when Gina came to London and there was the most appalling and distasteful scene you could conceivably imagine."

"Gina and I traveled from Paris to London together last Friday evening, as you know," he said as the taxi moved into Berkeley Square. "Lilian knew our arrival time, and, I suppose in the course of casual conversation, mentioned it to Eric, who for reasons best known to himself told Thérèse when she called to ask if he knew when I was returning to London. Thérèse went to the airport to meet me in her car, and found me with Gina. Naturally she thought the worst. She wanted to believe there was some other woman. It would have given her a concrete reason to explain why our engagement collapsed—she couldn't bring herself to believe that the fault was hers, not mine. Or perhaps it would be more accurate to say she couldn't believe that the fault was ours—that we were incompatible. If she could have believed I had found someone else, she could have blamed me for everything and exonerated herself. So, you see, she wanted to believe the worst of Gina.

"I needn't trouble you with the sordid details of the scene at the airport. It's enough to say that merely to end the scene I put Gina in a taxi to her hotel and took a separate taxi to my flat. I half expected Thérèse to follow me to resume the quarrel but I was expecting too much even of Thérèse. She called me up instead. I told her the truth—that there was nothing between Gina and me, and even if there was it was certainly no longer her business—and hung up without waiting for her to finish."

We crossed New Bond Street and raced eastwards to the perimeter of Mayfair.

"And you saw Thérèse on Saturday?" I said tentatively at last. "With Gina?"

"No," he said. "Gina never saw Thérèse on Saturday and I haven't heard a word from Thérèse since then. She hasn't even called me. Perhaps she's at last beginning to see reason." He took out his cigarette case and then changed his mind and replaced it in his pocket. We reached Regent Street and crossed it into Soho. "On Saturday," he said, "before I took Gina to lunch with the Jantzens, I apologized for the scene, but Gina was very good about it and we agreed to consider it forgotten. Then we had lunch with the Jantzens and went our separate ways."

"I see."

He said wryly to me as an afterthought: "Now you can understand why I sympathized with Gina when her ex-fiancé made such a clumsy attempt to win her back in Paris last week."

"Yes—yes, of course."

"Thérèse and I had been engaged three months, but I

92

soon realized we had made a mistake. We just weren't suited. It became extremely awkward."

I was not sure of what to say. In the end I said nothing, and as the silence lengthened he asked: "Did Lilian mention what happened?"

"About Thérèse? Yes, she said Thérèse was rather unreasonable—and a little jealous—"

"So she did tell you." He seemed more irritated than angry now; his eyes had an opaque, introspective expression. "Yes, Thérèse became convinced that there was something between Lilian and me. It was quite absurd because Lilian and I are business friends only and it's been that way ever since we first met. But Thérèse saw it differently. It so happened that after Thérèse and I became engaged Lilian and I had to be in Paris together for an exhibition and conference. It never even occurred to me that Thérèse would begin to be jealous of Lilian—of all people—but she worked herself into such a state of jealousy that she flew to Paris after us and found that we were both staying at my Paris *pied-à-terre*.

"I suppose that was rather foolish of us, since such a situation is open to misconstruction, but we had done it so often before that we thought nothing of it. I put up a folding cot in the office and Lilian had the sofa bed in the living room; it was economical and convenient, especially in the early days, when every penny counted with us. However, Thérèse immediately thought the situation could have only one possible meaning. I explained a dozen times that Lilian is a dedicated career woman and simply not interested in anything except her work, but I don't think Thérèse ever really believed me. After that things became steadily more impossible between us, until in the end I decided that there was nothing to do except call the whole thing off. Unfortunately I then discovered that Thérèse was so obviously enjoying her jealousy that she couldn't bear the idea of breaking up. It was all a little difficult."

The understatement might have made me smile in other circumstances but at that point I was too busy feeling guilty; I debated whether to tell him that he had misunderstood me and that the Jantzens had not mentioned Thérèse's suspicions of Lilian. Before I could make up my mind we arrived at the restaurant and the opportunity to speak was gone.

The restaurant was large and dignified and, despite the numbers dining, extremely quiet. After we had ordered I said impulsively: "It's very kind of you to keep taking me out to dinner like this, especially when you must have such a lot on your mind."

He looked surprised. "Do I seem to have so much on my mind?"

"Well, Thérèse—"

"She may be on the Jantzens' minds, but she's certainly not on mine." He smiled. "You're the one who has all the worries, not me, although I must confess I'm beginning to share your concern about Gina."

"I'm surprised you're not more worried about her than you are," I couldn't help saying. "I would have thought—"

"Listen," he said, interrupting, "I don't know what Gina told you in her letters but as far as I was concerned she was a delightful relief after Thérèse's melodramatics, a pleasant interlude to take away the bitterness Thérèse had left behind. I wasn't seriously interested in Gina and I'd be surprised if she was seriously interested in me."

"Why take such trouble to persuade me?"

"Because I can recognize skepticism a mile off." Our glances met for a split second of tension across the table and then he laughed carelessly, picked up his napkin and shook it out into a wide square. "And besides," he said, amused, "I'm anxious to prove to you that I'm not a mere philanderer to be regarded with extreme distrust."

My cheeks burned. "Have I given you the impression that that's what I think?"

But he refused to be serious. "Don't sound as if you have a guilty conscience!" He turned and signaled the wine waiter. Then, to me: "Will you have some wine with your roast beef?"

"No, thank you."

"No? Are you sure? Not even a glass?"

But I was adamant. The meal continued but the atmosphere was less relaxed than it had been the previous evening, and after the meal we did not linger over our coffee.

"Why don't we go to Scotland Yard?" said Garth suddenly. "I can see you're too worried about Gina to enjoy yourself. We'll go and see your friend—what was his name?—and report that she's still missing. And at the same time we can find out when she checked out of the hotel on Saturday."

Relief crept over me; I looked across at him thankfully, grateful for his understanding. "Would you mind? I'm sorry to be such bad company this evening, but—"

"Nonsense! And don't bother to apologize for anything—I can see now that I've been inconsiderate. We'll take a taxi to the Yard and get this straightened out without any more delay. Are you ready?"

I was. We left the restaurant and went out once more into the long, light, summer evening as dusk was beginning to fall. Presently we were in a taxi sweeping along the Embankment beside the river to Big Ben, Westminster and Scotland Yard.

Afterwards I felt better, even though Detective Inspector Fowles had been unable to help much except to go over the details of Gina's disappearance and to promise that further inquiries would be made. We also found out that Gina had checked out of her hotel *after* making the phone call to New York, and that she had checked out alone, unescorted, and apparently of her own free will.

"So she was all right when she left the Jantzen apartment," I said with relief. "But then why did she make the phone call? And why did she hang up as if she was interrupted?"

But there were no answers to these questions, only theories and suppositions. After thanking Fowles we left the Yard and made our way by taxi down Whitehall back to my hotel.

"I don't understand it," I said to Garth. "I just don't understand. Can she really have gone on to Rome, as the Jantzens suggested, to meet this Italian film producer? Why didn't she call me back to say everything was all right? Unless she had a memory lapse I can't believe she'd carry on exactly as if nothing had happened."

"Well, it's in the hands of the police now," Garth said. "If they can't trace her no one can. They'll find her."

He asked me if I wanted some coffee before returning to the hotel, and partly because I was dreading the moment when I would be on my own again without him, partly because I wanted to make amends for my preoccupied behavior at dinner, I agreed. We went to the London Hilton on Park Lane and had coffee on the second floor in the large, spacious lounge. The coffee, which was served American style, was reassuring and delicious. I began to feel better.

"I can't thank you enough for coming with me to the police tonight," I said to Garth. "I was dreading that visit but it all went off very well. I feel much happier now."

He smiled, shrugged his help away as if it were nothing. We began to talk of other things, and soon the time slipped away again until it was after midnight. I think he realized before I did that I was tired; we left the Hilton, found a cab and were driven off around the edge of Hyde Park Corner into Piccadilly just as my eyelids began to feel heavy and my head was starting to ache from weariness.

But I was happy.

He smiled at me in the darkness. "One day," he said, "when that tiresome girl Gina has stopped appearing and disappearing like the Cheshire Cat, you and I are going to go out again in London and have an evening like the one we had last night in Paris."

Everything blurred, tilted, melted into darkness as I closed my eyes. I could feel the material of his jacket straining across his back as he tightened his grip on me; his cheek grazed my own, his mouth was hard, the kiss smoothly painful in its intensity. I pushed him away dizzily, overcome by emotions which I could not even begin to cope with, but he was already relaxing his grip and withdrawing of his own accord.

We were silent. There was nothing to say. It was not as if this had been yet another casual kiss in the moonlight on the steps of the Sacré-Coeur. Now we were no longer casual. I felt committed, involved. Defensive barriers had become important, useless structures, shells behind which it was impossible to shelter any longer. There were no barriers any more and yet we were still apart, separate from one another, he with his thoughts, I with mine. And my thoughts said to me: Is he really honest? Is he really telling the truth? And instinct, untrammeled by the logic of the defensive barriers, in spite of everything persistently told me he was not.

I looked at him. His face was shadowed, silent, remote from me.

"What are you thinking?" I said suddenly and on an impulse reached out to take his hand in mine as if I could dispel my suspicions by touching him. His fingers, long and strong, interlocked themselves with mine. His mouth smiled at me faintly but left his eyes withdrawn, their expression unreadable.

"Why," he said, "I was thinking how odd it is that we've known each other less than forty-eight hours. I feel as if I've known you a very long time."

The taxi halted outside the hotel and he got out to escort me into the lobby. "I'll be in touch with you tomorrow," he said. "I can't manage lunch, I'm afraid, but perhaps I could see you later."

We kissed, parted; when I looked back at him I saw he was looking back at me too. And suddenly I forgot all my doubts and all my worries and remembered only that soon I would see him again.

I was awakened shrilly at eight by the ring of the telephone bell at my bedside. Half asleep I scooped off the receiver and pulled it on to the pillow beside me.

"Claire?" said Warren Mayne, sounding impossibly brisk and bright. "Hi, it's me. What's new? I tried to get you last night but didn't have any luck."

I made an enormous effort. "Maybe we could talk things over at breakfast? I can't think clearly at the moment."

"Breakfast? Sure. I'll meet you downstairs at nine."

When we met an hour later he was still bright and brisk and so obviously full of energy that I felt tired merely to look at him. "So what happened?" he demanded, starting to fire questions at me as we sat down to breakfast and I glanced at the menu. "Did you get anything more out of Cooper? Is there any other news?"

Over orange juice, cereal, toast and marmalade I told him about the Jantzens, my visit to Scotland Yard with Garth, and the news that Gina was alive and well after leaving the Jantzen apartment last Saturday. I also mentioned the Jantzens' suggestion that she might have flown to Rome to see an Italian film producer.

"Well, we can check that easily enough," said Warren at once. "What's his name?"

"Dino di Lasci."

"We'll call him up and ask him if he's seen Gina."

His energy must have rubbed off on me; by the time we left the dining room I had recovered myself and was willing to share his determination to follow every possible lead. We spent the next hour in his room while he put through a call to Italy and finally succeeded in speaking to di Lasci's secretary. She said she had never heard of a Miss Gina Sullivan, an American model from Paris.

"Could you check with your boss?"

She apparently gave an unsatisfactory reply.

"It's serious," said Warren. "This is the CIA. We have reason to believe Miss Sullivan was murdered."

I was disturbed by this gross distortion but Warren never turned a hair. "She's going to ask di Lasci right now," he said, pleased, to me. "I *thought* that would get results."

But it was all for nothing. Di Lasci came on the wire and said he had neither heard of nor seen Gina and that he was unable to help us.

Warren then called London airport and checked the flight lists to Rome the previous Saturday evening. There was no indication that Gina had ever made a reservation.

"I should have done that first," he said disgusted, "instead of wasting money on a call to Rome. Still, there's no harm in being thorough, I guess. Who shall we call up now? Who should we talk to? I'd like to speak to the Jantzens, but maybe I wouldn't learn any more from them than you learned yesterday."

"Probably not."

He thought for a moment. Then, suddenly: "You know who I'd like to talk to? Cooper's ex-fiancée Thérèse. It strikes me she's the only possibility we've got to explain Gina's behavior. If Thérèse came to the Jantzen apartment and created a scene—"

We argued about it for some time. I was extremely reluctant to meddle with Thérèse, but I had to admit that Warren's idea was reasonable enough.

"I can't see that it would do any harm to talk to her," Warren insisted. "She should be glad to meet me and find out that I want to get Gina away from Cooper as much as she does. You needn't come if you'd prefer not to, but—"

"Oh, I'll come with you," I said hastily. "But where does she live? I don't even know her last name."

"Call Eric Jantzen—he was pretty friendly, wasn't he? Call him and ask for Thérèse's second name. Then we can find her address in the directory."

"But what excuse am I to give?"

"Just tell him the truth—that you want to check with Thérèse to make sure she hasn't seen Gina since Gina disappeared."

Feeling nervous and ill at ease I dialed the number of the Jantzen apartment and found Eric at home. He was co-operative, appearing perfectly satisfied with my explanation. Thérèse's surname, he told me, was Mariôt.

Carried away by his helpfulness he also gave me her address and phone number.

"Great," said Warren, as I replaced the receiver. "Let's go."

"Without calling her?"

"She might put us off with some excuse. Let's take a cab and go over and see her in person."

I followed reluctantly in his wake.

It was about eleven o'clock by that time. The day was gray and overcast but there was no rain and it was comfortably warm. Piccadilly Circus looked sad in the morning light, after its multicolored splendors of the previous evening, and a crowd of tourists mingled with the down-and-outs who sat on the steps beneath Eros. We found a cab, and Warren, treating the cockney driver as if he spoke a foreign language, showed him the piece of paper on which he had written Thérèse's address.

We set off westwards again, our taxi nudging its way through the heavy traffic, and within twenty minutes were in Knightsbridge. At South Kensington Underground the taxi turned down the Old Brompton Road and finally made a left turn into a gracious square flanked by large white houses.

"Thirty-seven," yelled the driver through the glass partition and halted the cab abruptly.

We got out; Warren paid him slowly as if he were translating shillings and pence into dollars each time he pulled a coin from his pocket.

"Well, come on," said Warren, as the cab drove off again. "Let's see if she's here." He mounted the steps to the front door and examined the three bells on one side of the porch. Thérèse's name was printed on the top one. Warren pressed the knob, held it in position for a second and waited.

There was no reply.

"We should have called first," I said.

Warren didn't answer. He was busy rattling the door handle, but without success. I was just about to suggest that we go away and make no further to break into the building, when a voice behind us said: "Want any 'elp, dears?"

We spun around guiltily. Facing us was an exceedingly fat woman with very false teeth which she now displayed generously in a smile. " 'Oo are you wanting? If it's the French lady, she's gorn. Ain't seen 'er all week."

We were too taken aback to ask her who she was. She did not look as if she were the type of person who would live at that address but obviously she seemed well acquainted with the house.

"Is that right?" said Warren, stalling, and added clumsily: "Would you be the maid?"

"Maid!" She looked at him as if he were an anachronism from the last century. "Gawd 'strufe, no, dear. I come in and does for Mrs. Cheese in flat B three times a week and cooks the evening meal on alternate Sats." She pointed to the three doorbells. "Mrs. Cheese lives below the French lady."

I realized the language barrier had put out invisible fingers to confuse us. Warren had correctly guessed her rôle but had called it by the wrong name; this was one of the famous London charwomen, not an American maid.

"As it happens we did want to see Miss Mariôt," I said to her with a smile. "Do you know how long she'll be away?"

"Couldn't say, dear, I'm sure. 'Ere, are you American? I thought you was. I know all about America. We watch telly and see it on the films. Skyscrapers and big cars

102

and men with guns. My ole man says it'll be like that 'ere before long."

Warren was evidently torn between correcting her innocent impression of American life and finding out more about Thérèse. As he hesitated I said: "When did you last see Miss Mariôt? I mean, was it a long time ago, or—"

"No, last Saturday." She leaned her massive figure against the railing and settled down to enjoy herself. "It was one of my alternate Sats for Mrs. Cheese so there I was getting the dinner, all 'appy as a lark and singin' under my breath, and the sun was shining (makes a change, that does!) so I flings open the window and leans out to sniff the fresh air." She paused meaningfully. Feeling something was required of us we both nodded. "And suddenly, my Gawd, there she was—shouting and screaming something awful—"

"Miss Mariôt?" Warren asked.

"Course it was! 'Oo do you think I mean—my Mrs. Cheese? Mrs. Cheese don't carry on like that. Such a carry-on it was, I could 'ardly believe me ears. Well, there she was a-ranting and a-raving and making a to-do and she shouts out: 'I'll ruin you both!' she says all nasty-like, 'you and Lily both of you.' No, I'm telling a fib. It wasn't Lily she said. It was something else like it."

"Lilian."

"That's it! You know 'er? Lilian. Anyway, Miss Whatsit, the French lady, went on ranting about Lilian, and then 'er fiancé, a very nice gentleman called Mr. Cooper, said—"

"It was Mr. Cooper who was with her?"

"Course it was! I knows Mr. Cooper. Poor man, I felt sorry for 'im all tied up with that foreigner. I used to meet 'im on the stairs sometimes and twice 'e gives me a lift to the tube in 'is car. A very nice gentleman Mr. Cooper is . . . So where was I? Oh yes. So there was I all breathing in the fresh air, so to speak, and all this to-do going on over my 'ead, and Mr. Cooper says: 'Don't be a fool, Terezz,' 'e says, proper narked 'e was, and she shouts out something else and slams the door and I 'ears 'er footsteps pounding downstairs past my Mrs. Cheese's door and then the front door slams and she's gorn. And I ain't seen 'er since. Nor 'as Mrs. Cheese. Mrs. Cheese was saying to me only yesterday that she wished Miss Whatsit had cancelled 'er order of the French newspaper while she was away as it keeps being delivered and cluttering up the 'all downstairs. But it's plain to see what 'appened. She broke it off with 'er fiancé over this Lilian—whoever *she* is (and mark you I wouldn't blame that Mr. Cooper for taking up with someone else)—and then she went away to recover. No one thinks at times like those to cancel the morning paper. I told Mrs. Cheese so and Mrs. Cheese agreed."

We nodded, mesmerized into agreeing with Mrs. Cheese. I was trying to remember whether Garth had said he had not seen Thérèse since Friday night at the airport, but as far as I could recall he had merely said that Gina had not seen Thérèse since then. He hadn't mentioned himself.

"When was this?" I said unsteadily. "Saturday?"

"Saturday, it was. That's right. About six o'clock in the evening. I was all set to peel the potatoes."

And Gina had called me at nine-thirty, London time, that same night.

"Well, thank you very much, ma'am," said Warren politely. "You've been most helpful, and we're grateful to you. I guess we'll have to get in touch with Miss Mariôt in some other way."

"Good luck to you, I'm sure," said our informant agreeably and heaved herself up the steps to the front door. "I must be on my way to Mrs. Cheese. I 'opes you enjoy the rest of your 'oliday in England."

We chorused our thanks and began to walk away along one side of the square towards the Old Brompton Road.

"Should I have tipped her?" Warren asked, worried.

"Absolutely not."

"You think so? Maybe you're right. I wouldn't have known how much to tip anyway." He sighed, ran his fingers through his hair. "Boy, what a break! We sure were lucky meeting her like that. What did you make of it all? It certainly looks as if Gina wasn't the only one to disappear that evening, doesn't it? I'm convinced that Cooper's at the bottom of all this—hell, he was involved with both women and—if we can believe the maid—with his partner as well. Looks as if he was two-timing everyone on a grand scale."

I said levelly: "I'm quite certain he isn't having an affair with Lilian."

"Why?"

"Well, for one thing because he's on good terms with Eric."

"Maybe Eric doesn't know."

"After ten years?"

We walked on for a few moments. Then: "According to Garth," I said with studied indifference, "he was trying to avoid any romance with all three women, not to involve himself with them. He had broken his engagement to Thérèse. He was apparently unconcerned by the idea of Gina flying off to Rome to see a film producer. And there's no proof that he's ever had more than a business relationship with Lilian. He was trying to get away from Thérèse and Gina, not closer to them."

105

"Let's face it," said Warren ironically, "he succeeded. He got away from them so successfully that now no one can find them."

I didn't answer. I was feeling chilled, frozen with an ice cold pang of dread.

Presently Warren said: "Don't tell me you're hooked on him as well."

I still didn't answer.

"Wow!" Warren hooted. "He sure must have a way with women! I must study his technique the next time I see him."

"Oh, for God's sake, Warren!"

We reached the Old Brompton Road. "Okay," said Warren not unkindly. "You think Cooper's innocent and I think he's guilty. So what's the next step? Let's go back to the hotel and see if you have any messages from Scotland Yard."

Back at the hotel I found not a message from Scotland Yard, but a note to say that Eric Jantzen had called and could I call him back at his apartment.

I did not want to make the call with Warren breathing down my neck so I went to my room and said I would speak to him as soon as I had talked to Eric. Then, sitting on my bed. I dialed the Jantzen number and waited for Eric to answer the phone.

He sounded pleased that I had returned his call so promptly. "Have you heard any news of Gina?" he said. "Did you contact the police again?"

I told him how Garth and I had visited Scotland Yard the previous evening and he listened with interest. Then: "Look," he said. "Are you doing anything for lunch? Our flat is only a short bus ride from your hotel—could I come over and meet you?"

I managed to conceal my surprise. "Thank you very

much," I said. "That would be very nice."

"Good! I'll be over in about twenty minutes, then."

I hung up and then spoke to Warren on the house phone to tell him what had happened. He was as surprised as I was but agreed that it was possible I might discover something new. We arranged that I should give him a call later, on my return, and afterwards I had a few minutes in which to relax before I went downstairs to the lobby to meet Eric Jantzen.

He was already waiting for me. "There's a good little restaurant just off the Haymarket," he said. "It's not far. Hardly worth a cab. Would you mind walking, or—"

I said I wouldn't mind so we set off. He talked fluently enough as we traversed Piccadilly Circus and turned into the Haymarket amidst the lunch hour crowds, but I had the feeling he was making an effort. After we had exhausted the subject of the weather and the traffic problem in big cities we reached the restaurant, which was small and neat and obviously inexpensive, and went inside.

By this time I had formed the impression that he did not like to spend money. It occurred to me vaguely to wonder what his financial position was. Artists were notoriously poverty-stricken. I thought of his rich, clever wife and wondered why he tolerated her thinly disguised apathy towards him.

"Where did you first meet your wife?" I inquired over the minestrone. "Was it in England?"

"Ah, so you can tell I'm not English! I shall never lose the accent, it seems. No, Lilian and I met in Switzerland. I come from Altdorf, which is the little village near Lake Lucerne where our national hero William Tell was born. I was a young struggling artist who earned a living painting pretty empty little commercial pictures of the beautiful scenery. Lilian was a sympathetic tourist."

It seemed that Lilian felt compelled to help men less fortunately placed than herself. "I see," I said tentatively, not really understanding.

"We had a lightning romance and married two weeks later in Geneva." He smiled, shrugged his shoulders. "Lilian's family didn't approve, but we didn't care." His large, sad face lit up unexpectedly. "We were young—in love. Those were happy times. I liked London and settled down quickly. Soon I was painting as I had always wanted to paint, and not painting what other people wanted. Lilian was most—" he paused for the right word "—inspiring."

And rich even then, I thought. She must have supported them both from the beginning.

"Lilian," said Eric Jantzen, "is a very wonderful, very talented woman. She believed in me. She had faith. In the end when I had my small share of success, I always said it was due to her because she gave me encouragement and help when I most needed it."

I tried to picture Lilian in the rôle of the devoted inspiring wife, absorbed in her husband's work. The effort strained my imagination. I couldn't really see Lilian absorbed in any work except her own.

"She must know a great deal about china and glass," I said presently.

"Yes, she knows much more than Garth. Garth's a mere businessman." He dabbed his mouth delicately with his napkin and reached for his glass of water. "But he likes to think himself an authority on glass."

"Tell me, Eric," I said, looking at him with what I hoped was an honest appealing expression. "What is *your* opinion of Garth Cooper? You probably realize that I barely know him, but my sister evidently thought highly of him so I'm anxious to discover what kind of man he really is. I hesitate to ask you, but you've known him some time and you're obviously a person of mature judgment, so I know I can believe what you say."

As I had intended him to be, he was flattered although he tried to disguise his gratification. His face puckered between the eyebrows as he prepared to give his mature judgment.

"Of course," he said at last, "he's always been more Lilian's friend than mine."

I waited. Presently he added good-humoredly, as if it were all a joke: "Why, he's a salesman! And a good salesman: An excellent, successful salesman! He has a saleable product and he sells it in the cleverest possible way."

"China and glass?"

"A mere sideline!" He was still amused, still speaking lightly to mask his seriousness. "Garth's talent is in selling himself—not literally, of course! But he knows how to appeal to people, how to charm them, how to make them like him. He has a talent for playing the rôle which the English would describe as 'the nice chap'. But beneath the nice chap façade he's a hard, tough, able businessman. He doesn't deceive me. He may deceive others but he doesn't deceive me."

"He doesn't sound like the right man for Gina," I said with a worried expression. "I hope she's not in love with him."

"She was attracted to him," said Eric. "That's undeniable. But she was too young for Garth. I know the kind of woman he likes." He toyed with his soup spoon as if it suddenly held an irresistible fascination for him. "He likes mature, clever women, not empty-headed young girls barely out of their teens." He looked up guiltily.

"I'm sorry, I don't mean to slight your sister, who was charming, but—"

"I understand." I broke a piece off my roll and buttered it. "You mean Garth preferred women like Thérèse."

"Precisely." He began to eat again. "I like Thérèse," he said unexpectedly. "Lilian didn't, but then I hardly expected her to. Thérèse was quick, intelligent and striking—a passionate, intense, exciting woman. If I painted portraits—" He broke off with a smile. "But I don't! However, if I did, I would have wanted to paint Thérèse."

My jealousy, ridiculous but unmistakable, made it hard for me to listen to him saying how attractive Thérèse was. To change the subject I said with interest: "What sort of pictures do you paint, Eric? I'm sorry I'm so ignorant of your work—I believe you're famous here in London."

"Hardly famous!" he said brightening, and began to talk about himself with a shy, modest enthusiasm which, for some reason, I found touching. It turned out that he painted abstracts and had dabbled briefly with surrealism. I said I had seen an exhibition of Salvador Dali's work at the Huntington Hartford Museum in New York. We talked of art for a while, and as we talked he lost his air of bogus joviality so that I caught a glimpse of the person he must have been long ago, when he first met Lilian—a sensitive, vulnerable young artist dedicated to his work. I found it impossible to imagine how the prosaic, business-like Lilian could ever have understood him.

But perhaps she never had.

"You will tell me if you have any news of Gina, won't you?" he repeated as we parted in the lobby of my hotel some time later. "Lilian and I are both so anxious to know where she is and if she's all right. You will phone us, won't you?"

"Of course!" I assured him, and thanked him warmly for the lunch before going up to my room. I knew I should call Warren to report on the lunch, but I felt I had had my fill of Warren that morning and when I reached my room I put off the phone call and lay down on my bed instead.

Within ten seconds my mind had fastened itself stubbornly on Garth Cooper.

He had implied the previous evening that Thérèse's suspicions of Lilian had come to a head over three months ago, at the beginning of his engagement. I strained my memory to recall his actual words but was left only with the memory of what he had implied. It occurred to me that Garth was clever at implying facts without saying anything outright. Now on reflection I was certain he had given the impression that Thérèse's jealousy of Lilian was past history, whereas according to the charwoman it was very much a present episode.

And that doesn't make sense, I thought. By last Saturday Thérèse should have been quarreling with him over Gina, not over Lilian. Gina was surely the center of his attentions by that time.

I felt depressed by the possibilities of the situation and by Garth's ambiguous behavior. Above all I began to feel depressed about Gina again, and not merely in regard to her disappearance but in regard to her relationship with Garth. I moved restlessly to the window, stared outside, turned back towards the door once more. Finally on an impulse I picked up my handbag and went downstairs to the street, in an effort to dispel the agony of passive waiting by a burst of action. I had decided to go to Garth's office. Instead of wondering helplessly about his

111

ambiguities I could ask him about them directly instead.

His office was in Knightsbridge. I felt incapable of coping with the Underground system or even the buses at that stage, so I took another extravagant cab and sat back in the shiny leather seat as London slipped past my eyes.

I pictured an imaginary Guide, Philosopher and Friend, the rôle which I had assumed for so long with Gina. "Dear Claire," my imaginary friend wrote with cold asperity, " you are letting your innate good sense run away from you, I fear. Kindly note the following observations: (1) You should never run after a man—always wait for him to come to you. (2) Never interrupt a man at his office when he might be transacting important business. (3) Disassociate yourself from this man Garth Cooper who is almost certainly not to be trusted. What does it matter whether he implies untrue facts or whether he patently lies about them? The point is that he is probably not presenting an honest picture to you and may have been dishonest about other matters of which you are unaware. (4) Why should you, who seldom have a date at home, believe for one moment that Mr. Cooper is as infatuated with you as you (apparently) are with him? He has clearly been taking a romantic interest in you to blunt the edge of your inquiries into Gina's disappearance. (5) Should you wish to disassociate yourself from Mr. Cooper yet not know how to begin, there is one very simple remedy: don't see him again. (6) Pull yourself together and stop behaving so foolishly. Yours in disappointment . . ."

The cab hurtled into the Hyde Park Underpass and soared up again a moment later into Knightsbridge.

I can't help it, I thought, I love him. I can't help it.

The taxi drew up past Harrods and the driver pointed

across the road. "That's the building, Miss. Sorry you're the wrong side but no U-turns allowed here."

"Thank you," I said. I got out, paid the fare and crossed the street. There were office buildings above an exclusive row of shops, most of the windows displaying antiques. Inside the building there was an old-fashioned elevator. A board nearby told me that Garth and Lilian conducted business on the first floor, and after I had realized that the English say first when they mean second I avoided the elevator and walked up the stairs which wound around the shaft. The door marked "Cooper-Jantzen Limited, Importers-Exporters, China and Glass" was directly ahead of me. Suddenly wishing I had not come I walked up to the door and opened it before my nerve could desert me.

Inside was a light, airy, surprisingly modern outer office with thick green wall-to-wall carpeting and restful pale walls. A few feet away from them were two doors leading into rooms which I guessed were the partners' private offices; to my left I caught a glimpse of a file room and to my right was a gleaming desk, an electric typewriter and a very executive secretary with a curtain of jet black hair, blood-red fingernails and cool competent black eyes.

"Good afternoon," I said uneasily. "Is Mr. Cooper in, please?"

"Mr. Cooper is out of the office at the moment." She delicately adjusted a strand of hair. "Have you an appointment?"

"No—no, I haven't."

"I could make one for you." She opened a red leather appointment book. "What name is it, please?"

"Claire Sullivan, but this isn't a business matter. Could I wait for him, or is it unlikely that he'll return soon?"

"No, I expect him back at any minute." She glanced at her watch as if to confirm what she had said, and stood up and moved past me towards the file room. "Would you like to come this way, please?"

Beyond the file room was a tiny waiting room which looked out on Knightsbridge.

"If you'd like to wait here . . ."

"Thank you," I said.

She walked away gracefully, and I sat down and picked up one of the magazines on the table nearby. It was *Punch*. Presently I put it down and picked up *Paris-Match*.

Ten minutes passed. The phone rang twice and I could hear the murmur of the girl's voice as she took the calls. The electric typewriter chattered intermittently, but presently I heard her get up and come through the file room towards me.

"Would you like some coffee?" she inquired from the doorway.

"If you're making some."

"I always make some at three." She sounded bored about it. "Mr. Cooper and Mrs. Jantzen like strong black coffee after long business lunches."

In the file room she picked up a percolator and wandered into the outer office again. The front door opened, ringing the small bell hooked to the hinge, and slowly shut itself after her.

I was alone.

Standing up in an agony of restlessness I went out into the file room, examined the small photocopying machine, prowled around the file cabinets. In one corner was a closet with its door ajar. I glimpsed a man's raincoat hanging inside, and was just about to turn away when I caught sight of an envelope sticking out of one of the pockets. I wouldn't have looked at it twice if I hadn't

114

noticed that the only word visible to me of the address was written in purple ink.

I thought of the letters then, the notes from Hollywood, the reams from Paris. And all of them written in Gina's favorite shade of purple.

Quickly, smoothly, before I had had time to think twice, I took out the envelope. It was empty. He had evidently either destroyed the letter or put it in a safe place and then stuffed the envelope hurriedly into his raincoat pocket. I studied the postmark. The letter had been mailed in Dorking, Surrey, at three o'clock on Monday afternoon, two days after the phone call to me from the Jantzens' apartment, and there was no doubt at all that the purple-inked handwriting on the envelope belonged to Gina. . . .

7

I went on staring at that empty envelope in the silent deserted office. Somewhere far away beyond the windows of the waiting room came the muffled roar of the Knightsbridge traffic; everything close at hand was very still. Suddenly outside the office in the corridor I heard quick footsteps and I just had time to stuff the envelope back in the raincoat pocket before the door of the outer office was pushed open and Garth and Lilian walked in.

"Catherine? Damn it, where is the girl? We employ her to answer the phone, not to spend half the time in the cloakroom making herself look glamorous."

They could not see me. They were still in the adjacent outer office and I was shielded from them by the half open door of the file room.

"There's no need to be so hard on her—she's a very good secretary and the glamor is only put on for your benefit."

"My God, the next thing I know, Thérèse will be calling to accuse me of having an affair with my secretary!"

I had been about to step forward to announce my presence but the mention of Thérèse made me freeze to a halt.

"I must say, Garth, you're in a very bad mood this afternoon! I can't think why you're so upset about Thérèse when you haven't seen her for days—it's *I* who should be upset. Eric seems to have argued himself into believing that my behavior with you is suspect—"

"Oh, Lord!"

"Did you know that Thérèse saw Eric last Friday after you came back from Paris? He told me last night that there had been some sort of a scene at the airport with Gina."

"Scene! That's a mild word to use to describe such a sordid, embarrassing episode—"

"Why didn't you mention it to me before?" Lilian asked mildly.

"Why should I? Why should I bore you with the unfortunate incidents of my private life?"

"Apparently Thérèse told Eric on Friday, after the scene at the airport, that your interest in Gina was merely a smoke screen to conceal your interest in me."

"Look, I don't give a damn what Thérèse told Eric or what Eric thinks—" Garth's voice had risen in anger.

"Well, I do! I have to live with him!"

"I can't think why you bother! It's so patently obvious that you've nothing but contempt for him that I don't know why you don't leave him."

"I don't want to bore you with the details of my private life any more than you want to bore me with yours," Lilian shot back. "Besides Eric would be heartbroken if we separated."

"And you're being noble and considering his feelings? That doesn't sound like you, Lilian!"

"Listen, Garth." Lilian's voice had assumed the patience of an adult teaching a child to tell time. "The point is that it suits me to go on living with Eric at the moment. Never mind why. It's none of your business. Just take my word for it that I want to go on living with him, and that I was extremely annoyed to discover that Thérèse has apparently been seeing Eric and trying to make him as jealous as she is—"

"For God's sake, Lilian, why blame me? *I'm* not responsible for Thérèse! If Eric's jealous, ignore him. Let him be jealous! He can't prove anything against you because there's nothing to prove."

"It's very easy to give advice like that, but not nearly so easy to carry it out. I don't want Eric upset. Incidentally, just as a matter of interest, what game are you playing with that girl Gina? Where is she and why are you hiding her?"

"My dear Lilian," said Garth with what sounded like genuine astonishment, "what in heaven's name are you talking about? I haven't the remotest idea where she is, and I'm *not* hiding her. Why should I be? I haven't seen her or heard from her since we all had lunch together on Saturday."

My cheeks burned for him as his lies rang in my ears.

Tears, unwanted and inexplicable, pricked behind my eyelids.

Lilian was saying skeptically: "Weren't you having an affair with her?"

"Good heavens, no! Gina's for men of twenty-five and forty-five, not for men in their mid-thirties."

"Gina struck me," Lilian said slowly, "as being for men of all ages. Didn't she at least tell you where she was going after we all parted after our Saturday lunch?"

"No, I excused myself from her and went home to Half Moon Street. I told her I'd phone her later, but in the end I didn't. I was tied up with other matters."

"Thérèse?"

"No, I haven't seen Thérèse since the episode at the airport on Friday night."

Another lie. I thought of Mrs. Cheese's charwoman talking on the steps of the white house on the square. At six o'clock on Saturday evening Garth had been quarreling with Thérèse in her apartment.

"I was dead tired," Garth was saying. "I'd had a busy week in Paris with very little sleep. I rested till about seven and then wandered out into Shepherd's Market, where I had dinner at a small restaurant. I half wondered whether to phone Gina at her hotel, but I didn't. I didn't feel sociable and wanted to be on my own."

"Well . . . the whole business of Gina's disappearance is certainly very odd, that's all I can say. I suppose you had no word from her on Sunday?"

"No, I spent Sunday at the office."

"At the office? Here? On a Sunday? My goodness, you're getting to be as much a slave to your work as I am! I thought you were always the one who told me I should never work on Sundays?"

"I was puzzled over the Rémy contract—last year's, no

this. I couldn't quite work out why we paid so much tax on the profits."

"Oh, I can explain all that to you—it's really very simple. Why did you take over the Rémy contract this year anyway? I can't remember why we decided that. It would have been more sensible if I had handled it just as I did last year. Besides, what does it matter about last year's tax? That's all closed now."

"I had a tip that the Inland Revenue were on the warpath again against small businesses like ours. If we get any inspectors coming round I thought I should make quite sure that everything was in order."

"Well, of course it's all in order! You know how careful I always am—"

"Wait, I can hear Catherine coming back. Let's go into your office."

They opened one of the other doors leading off the outer office and moved quickly into the room beyond. Pulling myself together I left the file room and returned to the adjacent waiting room just as the secretary opened the door of the outer office and let it swing shut behind her. The small bell attached to the hinges murmured faintly and was silent.

"Catherine?" called Lilian in the mild gentle voice she had adopted when I had met her the previous evening. "Is there any coffee?"

"I'm just going to make some, Mrs. Jantzen. Mr. Cooper, there's a Miss Claire Sullivan waiting to see you in the conference room."

There was a long moment of absolute silence. I closed my eyes in an agony of embarrassment and prayed that when I opened them again I would be somewhere else. But I wasn't.

"Shall I—" The secretary hesitated.

"That's all right, Catherine. Thank you." He must have moved back into the outer office by that time for his voice was clearly audible. The next moment he was entering the file room and crossing the floor to the waiting room doorway beyond.

"Good afternoon," he said formally, and even before I could reply he had closed the door and we were alone together, just he and I and a thousand doubts in that quiet little room above Knightsbridge.

"This is a pleasant surprise," he said fluently as I found myself incapable of speech, "but I'm sorry you had to choose to call on us when you did. I suppose you were obliged to listen to Lilian and me indulging in some rather undignified bickering on subjects ranging from Lilian's nonexistent extramarital intrigues to the machinations of the Inland Revenue authorities. I apologize if we embarrassed you, but at least I can remember saying nothing I wouldn't have wanted you to hear."

I turned away, not answering, unable to meet his eyes, and stared out over London.

He moved towards me until I sensed he was standing behind my shoulder.

"What's happened?" he said abruptly. "What's the matter?"

My eyes were blind. "Nothing," I said. I did not trust myself to say any more.

"You've heard bad news about Gina?"

I shook my head. As he put a hand on my arm I turned away from him again and groped my way to the door.

"Just a moment," he said sharply. There was a note of uncertainty in his voice. "Just a moment. You must have come here for a reason. What was it you wanted to say?"

I remembered dimly that a long time ago, before I

120

had found out that he must know where Gina was, I had wanted to ask him more about his quarrel with Thérèse on Saturday evening. Now I knew the answer; as far as he was concerned the quarrel was a secret, to be concealed for private reasons. There was nothing I could do, nothing more I could say. My common sense had been correct in telling me I should never have come to his office; it had been a stupid, foolish, misguided step to take.

"I'm sorry," I said with difficulty. "It was wrong of me to come here and bother you. It really wasn't very important anyway. Please excuse me."

After a moment he said: "I don't understand."

I was incapable of speech again. I fumbled with the handle to open the door, but his hand closed on mine and stopped me.

"Please," he said quietly. "Please, Claire. You must tell me what this is all about. What's the matter? Was it something to do with the conversation I had just now with Lilian?"

I thought of the empty envelope in his raincoat pocket.

"No," I said, and found myself looking up into his eyes. He looked puzzled and worried. I was conscious of an overpowering urge to confide in him but I knew I must not. He had lied, not once but several times, and it was now no longer possible to trust him. With an effort so immense that I felt drained of all strength I said: "I think all this worry about Gina is depressing me more than I thought. I came here simply to talk to you and it wasn't until I was here waiting that I realized how selfish I was being in bothering you in your office. But before I could leave you came in with Lilian."

He looked at me steadily. His eyes were very clear. "Well, I'm glad you came," he said at last. "And I'm glad you turned to me when you were depressed. So why don't we sit down and talk about it? Never mind the office. That can wait. If you came here to see me, then why rush away again as soon as I appear?"

I shook my head helplessly. "No—really, Garth—I'd prefer not to talk here—" I broke off, reached out to open the door again.

"Look, Claire—"

"I can't explain—I just don't want to talk—"

"The hell you don't. Well, I do. No matter what you think I want to tell you that ever since we met—"

"I must go. Please—" I tried to open the door.

"—I haven't been able to stop thinking of you—"

"Oh don't, don't, DON'T—" My composure was fast fading.

"But Claire darling—"

I burst into tears.

"Oh God, I'm sorry . . . I don't know what's the matter with me. I've been so clumsy and hamfisted every time we meet—if it hadn't been for this wretched business over Gina—"

"We wouldn't have met at all," I said shakily, raking through the contents of my purse for a handkerchief.

"Here, have mine." He pressed a large white hankerchief between my fingers. I blew my nose, mopped ineffectually at my face, tried to gather together the shattered remnants of my self-control.

"I'm sorry," I said distantly at last. "I'm not myself. Please excuse me if I leave now."

"Let me get you a drink—"

"No, I want to take two aspirin and lie down. I've got a bad headache."

"I'll go down with you and get you a taxi."

"No—"

"I insist."

I was too exhausted to argue anymore. We went out through the fileroom into the outer office where the secretary regarded us with impenetrable black eyes behind her curtain of black hair. Outside in the street Garth hailed a cab and gave the name of my hotel to the driver, together with a ten shilling note.

"I'll phone you this evening," he said to me. "Perhaps if you're well enough we can have a quiet dinner together somewhere."

"I—don't know—"

"I'll phone you around six. Take care of yourself." He kissed me; I felt his lips brush my forehead as his fingers tightened on my arm, and the tears pricked at my eyes again. " 'Bye."

My lips moved but I could not bring myself to say goodbye. He closed the door, the taxi moved forward into the heavy traffic and I was alone. Leaning back against the leather upholstery, my mind blank with a dozen conflicting emotions, I stared out of the window and felt my cheeks burn once more with bitter, silent useless tears.

When I arrived back at the hotel I found three telephone messages asking me to call Warren when I got back. I tore them up. In the privacy of my room at last I drew the curtains and lay down for about five minutes, but presently I got up again and went over to the mirror to repair my make-up. I felt calmer now. It seemed unlikely that I would cry again during the next few hours. My head ached dully and my eyes felt sore, but otherwise I was conscious of nothing except a numbed apathy. I felt defeated. It was typical, I thought with a detached incredulity, that the one man whom I really fell for would turn out to be a double-faced, plausible liar. I was convinced now that he was having an affair with Gina and

123

that he knew where she was, and for reasons of his own was keeping her hiding-place secret while ostensibly pretending to help me with a hypocritical willingness.

There was no doubt at all that he had been playing a double game. And because I knew he had been playing a double game with me I had found the scene at his office particularly humiliating and shameful. He had summed me up, guessed that his best way of handling me was to adopt a suitably romantic approach and had then played his adopted role with great skill. I had been flattered, deceived, clay in his hands. He must have thought me an innocent fool.

The tears were just beginning to prick my eyes again and threaten to ruin my new makeup when the phone rang. I nearly didn't answer it, but then instead seized the opportunity to take my mind off my troubles. "Hello?" I said cautiously into the receiver.

"I was just about to call Scotland Yard to report *your* disappearance," said Warren, aggrieved. "Where the hell have you been? You said you would call me after your lunch with Eric Jantzen, and here it is—nearly four o'clock. I've been worrying myself sick about you."

"I'm sorry," I said. "I was delayed. Do you want to come over to my room? I've got a clue about where Gina may be and I want to talk it over with you."

"You have?" He was agog. "I'll be right over. Hold everything."

The line went dead. I sat on the edge of my bed and held everything, and a minute later he was knocking on the door. I let him in.

"How did you find out?" he demanded excitedly. "What happened? Where is she?"

I suggested he sit down and have a cigarette. "I went to Garth Cooper's office this afternoon," I said without

124

emphasis. "I was suspicious of him. He wasn't there when I arrived but his raincoat was. In the pocket was an empty envelope which had a postmark dated Monday, three days ago. It was addressed to Garth, the handwriting was Gina's and the postmark said it was posted at Dorking in Surrey."

Warren was so astounded that he dropped his cigarette. There was a great fuss as he snatched it up again and stamped at the carpet. Then: "So Cooper was lying all along! If she wrote to him Monday—"

"He would have got it on Tuesday, or yesterday, Wednesday. He must know where she is."

"Where did you say the postmark was?"

"Dorking, Surrey."

"Surrey's south of here, isn't it? Dorking shouldn't be too far away. Look, I've got a road map of England in my room. Let me just go and get it and we can check and see where this place is."

It turned out to be about twenty-five or thirty miles south of London.

"Looks as if it's a fair sized town," said Warren, pondering over his guidebook. "Why don't we get a train down there tonight and see what we can find out? We must be able to get there by train. It looks as though it should be in the commuter belt."

I hesitated, not certain what to do, my determination dulled by my apathy.

Warren was still browsing over the map. "Dorking . . . Guildford seems to be the nearest other big town. Hey, listen to these names! Abinger Hammer, Shere, Gomshall, Holmbury St. Mary—"

The pain of memory was so intense that I bit my lip. He looked up. "Something wrong?"

"Garth told me he owned a country cottage at Holmbury St. Mary. He goes down there at weekends."

"So that's it!" cried Warren. "So that's where she is! She's at Cooper's place in Surrey!" He closed the guidebook with a bang and scrambled to his feet. "Okay, let's go."

"Wait a minute," I said. "If Gina's staying in secret at Garth's country cottage she may not thank us for interfering. If she's capable of writing a letter and mailing it, it seems that she's there of her own free will and that apparently she's perfectly well and unharmed."

He stared at me. "What are you suggesting?"

"I think you know what I'm suggesting—you're not stupid. Listen, this is what I think happened . . ." I took a deep breath, summoned my will power, tried to speak in a cool, level disinterested tone of voice. "Gina traveled to London to spend the weekend with Garth, but they were met by an infuriated Thérèse at the airport. There was apparently a scene resulting in Gina and Garth traveling separately into central London, and naturally after that Garth would be afraid of Thérèse creating further scenes. So he suggested that Gina stay secretly at his cottage in Surrey."

"I don't believe it," said Warren at once. "He's been in London all week—what would be the point of Gina staying down in the country if she had traveled to London specifically to be with him? And why didn't she call Candy-Anna to tell her she wouldn't be returning to Paris for a few days? And anyway, you still haven't explained her call to New York from the Jantzens' apartment on Saturday night."

"Well then, you suggest another explanation which fits the fact that she's probably staying at his cottage in Surrey, unharmed, and of her own free will!"

He looked mutinous. His glance, roving around the

room as if for inspection, alighted on the telephone. "Let's call information and get the number of Cooper's home in Surrey."

"It won't have a phone."

"How do you know?"

"Why would Gina have written if she could have called him up?"

He was silent. "Well, let's give it a try anyway," he said at last. "There's no harm in trying."

"All right," I agreed doubtfully. After ten minutes of talking to various operators in both London and Surrey, he was told the house called Coneyhurst Cottage which belonged to Mr. Garth Cooper in Holmbury St. Mary was listed as having the number Holmbury 626.

"Could you try it for me, please?" said Warren at once.

More waiting followed. Then:

"No reply?" said Warren disappointed. "Thank you. I'll try again later."

"I suppose that's not altogether surprising," I said, trying to cheer him up as he replaced the receiver. "If Gina is hiding at the cottage she wouldn't answer the phone.

"True." He brightened a little. "At least I was right about the place having a phone. Well, what do you say, Claire? How about getting a train down to Dorking this evening, stopping overnight at a hotel there, and then hiring a car tomorrow morning to drive out to Cooper's house?"

I thought of Garth's promise to call later and to invite me to have dinner with him. If I were to speak to him, I thought, I would be weak and accept his invitation. And if I went out to dinner with him I would make matters even harder for myself than they were already. The best course I could possibly take would be to leave town for a day or two.

Warren was just beginning to look surprised by my hesitation when I said abruptly: "Yes, let's leave right away. How do we get there?"

"Let me talk to the people at the desk downstairs and see what they suggest. Then as soon as I get the details straightened out we can pack our bags and check out."

"All right."

After he had gone and I was alone I opened my suitcases and began to put my belongings inside once more. I found it a relief to have something to do, however mundane it was. Just as I was finishing, the phone rang and Warren told me there was a train leaving Waterloo Station soon after seven o'clock.

"We could have a snack here at five-thirty," he suggested, "and then get a cab to Waterloo. The trip takes about forty-five minutes. They've given me the name of a car rental agency in the town and the name of a hotel where we can stay, so now we're all set to go."

After we had had dinner we went to the desk to pay our bills, and I found that there was a phone message for me to say Garth had called. I tore it up and threw it away. Ten minutes later, with our luggage stowed safely into our taxi, we were leaving Piccadilly Circus on our way to Waterloo.

We reached Dorking shortly before eight and took a taxi to the inn which had been recommended to Warren at the hotel desk in London. I think we were both amazed by Dorking. Even Warren, who had never seemed to me to be very aware of his surroundings, was silenced by the wide High Street with its rows of old shops and narrow winding side streets packed with little pubs and antique stores. Our taxi driver informed us that our hotel had been a coaching inn in the old days, and suddenly I remembered a scene in Dickens' "Pickwick Papers" and knew why the name Dorking had seemed familiar.

"Would you believe?" marveled Warren as the taxi turned off the High Street under an ancient arch into the courtyard around which the inn was built. "People *live* here. It wasn't built by Walt Disney. People really *live* here."

And it was there at last that I felt I was in England. London with its vast modern buildings and cosmopolitan atmosphere had vaguely disappointed me, particularly after my brief visit to Paris, but here in Dorking I was no longer disappointed. As I entered my room and looked out of the window towards the large green hill which rose up above the town in the northeast, I had one of those curious, inexplicable moments that made me think I had been in here before. But that was nonsense. No town I knew in New England bore any resemblance to this old market town in Surrey, and none of my ancestors had come from England; my mother's family was Scottish and my father had been an Ulsterman from protestant Northern Ireland. I was a stranger here, and yet in spite of that I felt at home.

We were just in time for dinner; I had yet to get accustomed to the rigidity of English meal times and their inflexible hours. We ate an enormous English meal which seemed to my transatlantic ideas of finance to cost very little money, and afterwards we felt so replete we had to spend an hour in the lounge over our coffee before we could lever ourselves out of our chairs. Finally Warren went off to try to call the cottage again, but he was unsuccessful and in the end we decided to have an early night before driving out to Holmbury the following morning.

I spent an uneasy night. Supposing, I thought, Gina was indeed at the cottage, as it now seemed likely that she was. The scene would have to be handled with great care, and the more I thought about it the less eager I felt for Warren to be there with me. Warren would charge into the cottage like a bull in a china shop and besiege Gina with questions and demands and accusations. And supposing Gina decided not to come away with us but to remain at the cottage? Warren, who had been living on tenterhooks for longer than I had, might lose his head and do something stupid. I could almost visualize him carrying Gina off by force under the sincere conviction that he was acting for the best. I shuddered. Somehow I must contrive to arrive at the cottage before he did.

The next morning at breakfast I found he had already hired a car and intended to collect it directly after we had finished eating.

"I hate to tell you this," I said apologetically, "but I'm not feeling too well. Could we possibly postpone the trip until this afternoon? I've got a terrible headache."

He looked concerned. "Do you have any aspirin? You'd better go and lie down. Can I get you a doctor?"

"No, no," I said hastily before he could get carried away by consideration. "I'll take two aspirin and lie down and I'll be fine by noon. I'm sorry to postpone the trip, but—"

"That's okay, I understand. Don't worry about it— I'm just sorry you're feeling bad." He thought for a moment. "Maybe I'll drive out there on my own this morning and see if Gina's there."

"Please," I said with great restraint, "please let's wait till this afternoon! I've come over three thousand miles to find Gina and when we do find her I want to be there, not stretched out on a hotel bed."

He looked sheepish. "Sure, I understand. I'm sorry."

I silently heaved a sigh of relief. He decided to explore the town for a while and send some postcards to his friends, and after he had collected the car from the garage he prepared to set off on foot from the hotel.

"You can leave the keys with me," I said. "I don't want you losing them on your travels."

"Good idea," he agreed, completely serious although I had spoken lightly. "I'm always losing things."

He handed over the keys docilely and departed.

As soon as he was out of sight, I slipped out to the car, fitted the keys in the ignition and examined the controls. When I had lived at home I had driven a car every day of my adult life until all my reflexes and reactions were automatic and made without conscious effort; that was more than three years ago but I had driven rented cars occasionally since I had been living in New York, and had found that for me driving had become like swimming: once learned the skill is never forgotten. Driving a car in England would be different, I reasoned, but not difficult. Presently, after making sure I knew what I was doing, I started the engine, adjusted the shift and released the brake. The car trickled forward over the inn's cobbled courtyard. Soon I was easing my way carefully through the narrow arch and turning into the High Street. Dimly aware that I was more nervous than I had anticipated I crept along behind a green double-decker bus and found myself taking a right fork at the bottom of the High Street and driving on out of the town into the quieter residential districts. I stopped at the first gas station I came to and asked the way to Holmbury St. Mary. To my surprise I learned that I was on the right road.

"Keep straight on," said a solicitous mechanic. "Through

Westcott, past the Wotton Hatch Hotel. Keep going. Stick on the main road until you get almost to Abinger Hammer. Then as soon as you catch a glimpse of watercress beds on the left, watch out for a left turn. There's a white signboard just before the clock at Abinger which says 'To Holmbury St. Mary.' Take that left turn and drive another couple of miles or so and you'll be right in the village."

I thanked him and drove on. After a small village which I presumed was Westcott, the road ran deeper into the country, now and then cutting through sandy soil. I noticed the lush green of the foliage and glimpsed a range of hills beyond the fields to the north, but the traffic was much heavier than I had expected and it was impossible to look at the scenery as closely as I would have liked.

At last I found the side road past the watercress beds and turned left to Holmbury St. Mary. The country road was narrow and winding; there was little traffic now and I was able to take more notice of my surroundings. After passing through a hamlet where the cottages were so old and pretty that I nearly missed my way as I stared at them, I finally came to a larger village with a green, a church on a hill and some assorted houses and shops.

I stopped beside the nearest passer-by and asked the way to Coneyhurst. She said she had never heard of it. Discouraged I drove on and stopped at a pub; the pub itself was closed but the landloard was sweeping out the bar.

"Excuse me," I called through the open window. "Can you tell me where Coneyhurst Cottage is?"

He was a tall solid man with a moustache. "Coneyhurst?" He stroked the moustache absently. "Sounds as if it should be up Holmbury Hill. Who lives there?"

"A Mr. Garth Cooper."

"Ah!" He looked pleased. "Yes, I know Mr. Cooper. He often comes here weekends. The cottage is nearly all the way up the hill, an isolated spot with a good view. Take the road to Peaslake up the hill—you'll pass several big houses including Holmbury House itself. Keep following the signs to Peaslake, and just before you get to the top of the hill you'll see the cottage on your left."

I thanked him and returned to my car. The sun came out as I took the road uphill away from the village, and the light slanted through the tall trees with their brilliant green leaves and fell in patterns on the twisting narrow road. Presently the trees ended and the slopes of the hill rose steeply above me on my right. The view to the left was already worth pausing to look at, but I was too near my journey's end now and didn't stop. I passed occasional houses, including the gates bearing the inscription "Holmbury House," and swung uphill even more steeply. There was a fork in the road; I took the turn to Peaslake, as the landlord had instructed me, and ground the shift into a lower gear. I was glad Warren had hired a small Austin. The road was now so narrow that any larger car would have been nerve-wracking to drive.

I was just thinking that sooner or later I must surely reach the summit of the hill when I came upon the cottage. I had expected it to be old and quaint with a thatched roof, but I was disappointed. This was a small house, probably no more than thirty years old, and was perched firmly on the steep hillside looking out over a panoramic view across the valley below.

Parking the car off the road among the trees I got out and went slowly over to the house. All the windows were closed; there was no sign of life. I found the front door, and after a moment's hesitation rang the bell, but no one answered and presently I moved on around the house and tried the handle of the back door. It was locked. I stood there and wondered what to do. There was a small gardening shed a few yards from the house and for no reason other than curiosity I walked over and opened the door, but there was no one inside—only a few gardening implements and a wheelbarrow. As I turned away the sun went behind a cloud suddenly and a chill breeze swept up from the valley.

I shivered.

The blank sightless windows of the house stared at me, and suddenly, without knowing why, I was frightened. I retreated, moving quickly down the little terraced garden, and on the last terrace beside the hedge which marked the boundary of the grounds I noticed that part of an overgrown, weed-strewn flowerbed had been recently dug and hoed. The damp earth gleamed in the bright morning light.

I stared at it, refusing to recognize it for what it looked like. The patch was about six feet long and three feet wide. Suddenly, hardly aware that I was moving, I was halfway back to the shed. When I reached it I took the spade which was leaning against the wall and went back to the flowerbed at the bottom of the garden.

The spade sank softly into the wet earth and stopped.

I felt horribly cold. Presently I began to shiver again. Then, overcome with an obsession to see all my worst nightmares spring to the most appalling life, I stooped and scraped at the earth until at last I had uncovered a monstrous, distorted, gross object which I only just managed to identify.

It was a human hand.

8

After I had finished being sick, I steeled myself to go back to the grave again. There was something I had to find out, something I had to know. When I had finally achieved a state of mind resembling detachment I knelt down on the ground again and bent over the hand, my nose and mouth pressed against my handkerchief. There was a ring on the engagement finger, a brilliant diamond ring which sparkled mockingly in the bright light. I shut my eyes very tightly and then opened them again. It was still there. For several repulsive seconds I thought I would check to see if the ring bore any inscription, but I gave up the idea and retreated from the grave. The engagement ring was proof enough; Thérèse had not wanted to break off the engagement and it was possible she might have continued to wear the ring even after Garth had tried to end matters between them.

The full meaning of my discovery suddenly hit me in an overwhelming wave of shock. Garth's ex-fiancée was buried in the garden of Garth's weekend cottage. And Garth had been one of the last people to see her alive. After she had quarreled with him and stormed out of her apartment, her neighbors had not seen her again.

If the police knew the facts, I thought to myself, they could not help but think Garth was guilty of murder. She was making trouble for him, he had quarreled with

135

her, he was the last person to see her alive . . .

There was ice on my forehead. On reaching the shed I found a tap used for the garden water hose and turned it on. Cold water sluiced out. After washing my hands with a fanatical thoroughness, I dried them on the full skirt of my dress and went outside again into that cool morning light. Back in the driver's seat of the car I sat down and started to tremble from head to toe.

I tried to accept the fact that Garth was a murderer but my mind balked at such an idea. I was prepared to accept that Garth had been playing some sort of game where I was concerned but I could not believe that the game included murder. I tried to think clearly. Where had Thérèse gone after her quarrel with him last Saturday in her apartment? If he did kill her, when had it taken place, and where? And why bury the body in the garden of his own cottage when he could have chosen a site anywhere on the surrounding hillside?

I could not believe he had killed her. No matter how absurd and how lunatic my reasoning might be, I could not believe he was a murderer.

My thoughts, jumbled and confused, went on and on and on. I wondered if Gina had been in some way involved in the murder. If Garth were shielding Gina—no, Gina wouldn't have killed Thérèse. I wondered for the hundredth time where Gina was and wished with all my heart that I could somehow get in touch with her, and as I thought of Gina, I thought with a stab of dread of Warren.

I caught my breath. If Warren came to the cottage and found the grave in the garden, he would instantly contact the police. Somehow I had to prevent Warren from following through with his plan to investigate the cottage that afternoon.

The problem of how I could succeed in deflecting Warren from an apparently unavoidable course of action filled my mind as I made my way back to Dorking, but by the time I had arrived in the courtyard of the inn I was no nearer a solution than I had been when I had left Holmbury St. Mary. I glanced at my watch. It was eleven-thirty. Praying that I wouldn't meet Warren on the stairs or in any of the lounges I slipped into the hotel and hurried upstairs to my room.

With the door tightly closed and bolted behind me, I sat down on the bed, reached for the phone and asked the operator to put through a call for me to Garth's office in London.

I once read somewhere that a person in love can be considered to be temporarily unbalanced while the effects of the malaise linger in the mind. Certainly if anyone had ever told me a month previously that I would not report a dead body to the police as soon as I found it, but would instead phone the probable murderer to warn him of the danger he was in, I would have replied indignantly that I would never be so patently insane.

But I was. To make matters worse I was convinced that I was doing the only sane thing I could possibly do, since I had already persuaded myself against all the evidence that Garth was innocent. I sat waiting tensely in that still quiet bedroom as my call was connected, and then suddenly Garth's secretary Catherine had picked up the receiver and was saying in her cool, studiously polite voice: "Cooper-Jantzen Limited—good morning, may I help you?"

"Yes," I said rapidly. "Is Mr. Cooper there, please? This is Miss Sullivan."

"I'm afraid neither Mr. Cooper nor Mrs. Jantzen will

be in the office today. Is there any information I can give you?"

"Do you know where they are?"

"They've arranged to have a business weekend-entertaining French clients at Mr. Cooper's cottage in Surrey. Mrs. Jantzen went down to the cottage last night to get everything ready and Mr. Cooper was to go to the airport this afternoon to meet the clients' plane. It's possible that if you tried his flat you might just catch him before he leaves—do you have his number?"

"No—I only have the office number. Could you give it to me, please? It's very urgent."

"One moment," I heard her flick open an automatic telephone book. "Yes, it's Mayfair—that's MAY— 75432."

"Thank you very much indeed." I replaced the receiver and instantly picked it up again to give the operator the new number. I waited while she dialed and heard the bell ring endlessly at the other end of the wire.

"Sorry," said the operator. "There's no reply."

"Thank you." But I could not believe I would be unable to contact him. Springing to my feet in a fever of activity I left my room and went downstairs to the pay phone which I had noticed earlier outside the lounges.

By a miracle I had the right coins. After skimming through the instructions, which seemed unnecessarily complicated, I dialed the series of numbers and waited. The line began to ring and I thought in a panic: did I dial correctly? And such was my state of mind that I convinced myself in the space of three seconds that I had mis-dialed. I hung up, got my money back and began again.

This time, by some extraordinary miracle, someone picked up the phone on the first ring.

"Hello?"

I had opened my mouth, drawn breath to speak, but now I was struck dumb before I could say a word.

For it was not Garth who had answered the phone. It was Gina. . . .

"Garth?" said Gina, suddenly fearful as I did not reply, and I realized dimly that I must have stumbled on a prearranged telephone signal which enabled her to know when it was safe to answer the phone. "Garth, what is it? What's happened now?"

"What's happened now," I said shakily, "is that your sister has finally managed to track you down. Where the *hell* have you been?" Tears of relief were hot on my cheeks; the room swam in a dizzy mist of thankfulness.

"Claire! Oh God, where are you? What are you doing? Claire, I feel so bad about you, so terrible—"

"So you damn well should! I've been worrying myself silly about you and tying myself in the most impossible knots ever since you called!"

"I tried to call you back on Monday from Garth's apartment here but you'd already left New York—you left so *quickly,* Claire! I never, never thought you'd be on your way to Paris within two days—"

"What did you think I'd do, for heaven's sake? Dither about in New York while I wondered all the time if you'd been murdered or raped or kidnapped? Or stand rooted to the floor of my apartment like the Statue of Liberty while I waited for you to remember to call back?"

"I didn't forget you, Claire, I did actually try to call you back on Saturday night but your line was busy all the time, and after that I didn't get the chance to call till Monday, and by that time—"

"Why did you call from the Jantzen apartment?"

"I—look, I can't talk on the phone. Garth would be

furious if he knew I'd even spoken to you. He said absolutely no one, not even you, must know where I was until Saturday—"

"But look, Gina—you must tell me more! Garth's in trouble. His ex-fiancée—"

"I know."

"But—"

"Please, Claire darling, please—not on the phone. Listen, where are you? At the Regent Palace?"

"Dorking."

"Dorking! But you mustn't stay there! You—you'll be in danger—quick, come back to London. Come back at once. Get the next train to Waterloo. Don't ask questions, darling, just *leave*. Do you understand? Leave right away and come here."

"Yes, but just a minute! Where *is* Garth? I must talk to him. There's so much I—"

"He's on his way by car down to the cottage at Holmbury St. Mary. But Claire, you must come to London at once. Please! You must come!"

"Yes," I said to pacify her. "Yes, I'll get the next train. Don't worry."

"I'll be waiting for you," she said with relief. "And *hurry!*"

"What do you think I've been doing ever since your wretched phone call on Saturday night? All right, I'll hurry—don't worry, and take care of yourself."

"You too, darling. 'Bye now."

" 'Bye." I hung up, leaned weakly against the wall and fumbled for my handkerchief. I succeeded in finding the one which Garth had given me the previous afternoon at his office. It occurred to me wryly that I had cried more in the past two days than I had cried during the preceding two years.

140

When I had recovered myself, I went back upstairs to my room and began to consider what I should do next. I had every intention of joining Gina as soon as possible, but first of all I had to prevent Warren from going out to the cottage to find her, and then I had to try to see Garth to settle matters between us once and for all. But my first task was Warren. Presently I went to his room and knocked on the door, but there was no answer so I assumed he was still out on his walking tour. It seemed that he was making his tour of Dorking in great detail.

I tried again, a quarter of an hour later, and this time I had more success.

"How are you feeling?" he said as he let me into the room. "You don't look too good."

I could hardly have had a better opening. "Well, no, I still don't feel very well," I said listlessly. "Such a nuisance . . . But I've got some wonderful news for you—I've been trying to find you for the past half hour. What do you think happened while you were out? I called Garth's office to see if he had any news of Gina and would you believe it, who should come to the phone but Gina herself! I was so amazed I could hardly believe it! She refused to talk much on the phone, but we arranged to meet at five in the Regent Palace lobby."

"I don't believe it!" said Warren amazed. "She did? But what was she doing at Cooper's office? Where has she been?"

"I told you—she wouldn't talk on the phone! But isn't that marvelous news? I'm going to go on resting here for a couple of hours to get rid of my headache and then we can get a train to London to meet her at five o'clock."

"Why, that's wonderful!" he exclaimed. "Great! Let

me call up the station and find out the times of the trains to London—"

"You can go straight on up to London, if you like. But I just want to rest for a little longer—"

"Sure, I understand. I'll wait for you, though, and we can travel up together." He moved over to the phone. "Let me call now and find out the times of the trains."

I thought it unwise to argue with him further for fear of arousing his suspicions. If he decided to wait for me I could always give him the slip, just as I had that morning, and drive off on my own in the car. I heaved a sigh of relief, and as he began to talk into the receiver, I wandered casually over to the dressing table and picked up one or two of the objects which he had left scattered around on the polished surface. There were several postcards of Surrey.

I began to glance at each of them.

"Four forty-five? I see . . . and the one before that?"

His passport lay beside the postcard. I glanced at his photo and saw to my surprise that unlike most passport photographs, it was flattering. He looked young, bold, quick-witted and handsome as he stared defiantly into the camera. I flicked through the pages to the visa section to see which countries he had visited. A trip to Brazil was recorded for the previous year. Then his arrival in Paris and the visit to London.

"Okay . . . fine. Now what time does that reach London? It it an express?"

I stared. The visits to England and France appeared to be in duplicate.

"Just one stop, did you say?"

I went on staring. Presently I realized that the first stamp of the British Immigration Authorities was dated the previous Saturday and that the second stamp of the

French authorities was dated a day later on the Sunday.

Warren had been in London on the night Gina had made the phone call from the Jantzen apartment. He had been in London on the night Thérèse had disappeared. Warren had been in London on Saturday and had slipped back to Paris quietly on Sunday, and he had never once mentioned it to me. . . .

"Thank you very much," he said suddenly from behind me. "Goodbye."

He dropped the receiver and I dropped the passport; the noise of the one muffled the sound of the other. Feeling nothing but an amazed, uncomprehending bewilderment I turned towards him with a blank expression. "Is it all right?" I asked naturally. "What train do we get?"

"There's one that leaves at three and I suggest we get that. Why don't I pick you up at two-thirty?"

"Fine. Thanks, Warren," I said automatically, and feeling blank with shock, I left the room and went outside to the quiet corridor beyond.

When I reached my bedroom again I was still incapable of thinking clearly about my discovery but gradually as I stood by the window of my room and stared out over Dorking my initial shock began to recede. Why had Warren been in London? And why should he have concealed his visit unless he had something to hide? Could he conceivably have had any connection with Thérèse's murder? I spent several minutes thinking of Warren and remembering how I had always dismissed him as a naïve, ingenuous, overgrown adolescent. Apparently I had severely underestimated him. It seemed as if he were not nearly so naïve and frank as he appeared to be.

Another thought occurred to me. Might I not also be mistaken about Warren's single-minded determination to find Gina? I had been amused and touched by the devotion which had made him decide to take a week's absence from his work and fly to London to find her, but supposing his determination concealed a more sinister motive? I thought of Thérèse again, and suddenly I was saying to myself: supposing Warren killed Thérèse and Gina saw him do it. He'd want to find her at all costs once he realized she had witnessed his crime. And perhaps he had not known that she had witnessed the murder until I had arrived in Paris with my tale of Gina's distraught phone call to New York on Saturday night . . .

My thoughts seemed to be racing out of control. I tried to apply a mental brake. There was, I told myself, no reason why Warren should have killed Thérèse. Why *should* he have killed her? As far as I knew, they had never even met.

I began to wander restlessly about the room, and picked up my handbag irresolutely before putting it down again and returning to the window. Perhaps I was being dramatic in assuming Warren wanted to find Gina in order to silence her. Perhaps Thérèse had threatened Gina and Warren had killed her, accidentally or otherwise, in order to protect Gina herself. Then, when I had arrived in Paris and he had discovered from my information that Gina, unknown to him, had witnessed the crime, he had immediately tried to find her to explain the situation. If this theory were correct it would also explain why Gina had not gone to the police, for if Warren had killed Thérèse for her sake, Gina would hardly have wanted to call in the police.

I pulled myself together. I could stay in my room and imagine all kinds of theories, but that would hardly be the most sensible thing to do. The best course I could take would be to find Garth and demand that he tell me the whole truth without half-truths or evasions; since he had been hiding Gina in his London apartment and, before that, at his cottage in Holmbury St. Mary, he must presumably know why and from whom Gina wanted to hide.

My mind was made up. Moving quickly I picked up my handbag again, opened the door cautiously and slipped downstairs to the car, which was parked in the courtyard. The next moment I was in the driver's seat and edging the car out into the High Street as I began my return journey to Holmbury St. Mary.

I was so nervous that at first I took the wrong road out of Dorking and wasted precious minutes crawling through side streets while I tried to get my bearings. Finally, more through luck than judgment, I found myself on the road to Westcott and Abinger Hammer, and after some minutes I was driving past the hotel at Wotton Hatch which I had noticed earlier. It was beginning to rain; by the time I reached the turn to Holmbury St. Mary I had to use the windshield wipers. But the shower passed and as I took the road at last up Holmbury Hill to Garth's cottage, the sun shone palely again and the rain was a mere dark cloud shadowing the road behind me.

I was driving too fast. I had to will myself to slow down. Normally the narrow winding road would have been enough to persuade me to reduce my speed to walking pace but I was so anxious to see Garth and learn the whole truth of the situation that I was forgetting even the most basic rules of highway safety.

Fortunately I met no cars coming down the hill as I went up so I arrived at the cottage without incident. But even before I could park the car I knew that this time I would not be alone at the house; a sleek creamy Jaguar had stolen my parking place, the spokes of the wheels glittering in the sunlight, the hood thrusting gently into the undergrowth which crept up from the ground to meet the bumpers. Someone had arrived before me. I was just assuming that it must be Garth when it occurred to me that I had never seen his car before. In London we had always taken cabs everywhere. Supposing the car belonged to someone else? I hesitated, shivering violently as I remembered the dead hand in the shallow grave, and then pulling myself together, I let the car roll back a few yards and parked it off the road below the Jaguar. It must be Garth who had arrived at the cottage. After all, Gina had said that he was on his way. I was becoming neurotic, imagining danger where none existed.

I got out of the car and slammed the door shut. Everywhere around me it was very quiet. On my right the wooded hillside was still and motionless. Not a breath of wind whispered through the branches of the trees; a bird sang briefly and darted into the silent undergrowth. I was alone, part of the stillness of the landscape as I stopped to listen, and when I moved forward again I felt the damp twigs crunch beneath my shoes and my breathing quicken in my throat.

All the windows of the house were still closed; there was no sign of life. For a long moment I hesitated by the roadside and then with an effort I stepped off the road and walked swiftly up the path to the front door. I touched the bell, waited. The bell seemed to ring far away, a small faint trill of sound piercing the pall of silence. I went on waiting. I was just about to ring again when he opened the door.

His face was empty of expression. He looked at me as if he didn't know me.

"I'm sorry," I said stammering, "but I must talk to you, Garth."

146

He said nothing. He was very still, one hand on the latch, the other a tight fist at his side. As so often happens in moments of great stress I found myself noticing trivial things, that he was wearing casual clothes, dark slacks, blue shirt and, oddly, quiet-soled tennis shoes. His hair was untidy, and as I stood there watching him he smoothed it back with his hand in the old gesture which I had noticed when I had first seen him in Paris.

"I can't talk now," he said abruptly. "It'll have to be later."

"But—"

"Go back to London and I'll get in touch with you there."

I shook my head dumbly.

"Look, Claire, I'm sorry, but I can't talk now. I've got guests arriving any minute and I'm not ready for them. You'd better go back to London."

I was stung by his air of polite impatience, his attitude of thinly veiled exasperation. "To London?" I said quickly. "And where shall I wait in London? At the hotel? Or with Gina at your apartment?"

He stared at me. It was impossible to guess what he was thinking. Then: "Whichever you prefer," he said without expression, and began to close the door. "And now if you'll excuse me—I apologize for being so abrupt, but—"

"Don't bother to apologize," I said, infuriated by the fact that he was no longer even pretending to be interested in me, "because I'm not going." My eyes were pricking with the sickness of disillusionment, but my anger overcame my disappointment and wretchedness. I knew now that his interest in me had been assumed from the start to make it harder for me to find Gina, and some perverse, foolish streak of pride made me want to prove to him that he had meant no more to me than I had to him.

"Claire—"

"No," I said, my eyes hot with unshed tears. "No, you're going to listen whether you want to or not! Why did you tell me all those lies? Why did you tell me you hadn't seen Gina since Saturday when all the time you knew where she was? And why did you say you hadn't seen Thérèse since Friday at London airport when you quarreled with her at her apartment on Saturday evening? You lied and lied—"

"Listen," he said, white to the lips, "listen, Claire. Thérèse is dead—"

"Yes!" I cried. "Murdered! And buried over there in *your* garden!"

He opened the door a little wider and I thought he was going to let me into the house to talk to him but he merely moved out on the step beside me.

"I didn't kill her," he said slowly. "You must believe that. I didn't kill her."

"Why should I believe you!" I stormed at him. "You've told me nothing but lies from start to finish—"

"That's not true."

"It *is* true!"

"Oh, for God's sake!" he exclaimed, as if I had touched him on the raw. "Stop shouting accusations at me as if I committed a mortal sin! The only reason I lied—"

"—was to deceive me," I said. "I expected you to be honest with me and instead you—"

"I omitted certain facts—just as you did when you first met me. It was a long time before you told me what Gina had actually said during her phone call to you in

148

New York! If omitting facts makes me a liar, then you're as much of a liar as I am!"

"I—"

"Please," he said. "Go back to London. Go to my flat. See Gina and talk to her. I can't talk to you now."

"I was so worried about Gina!" The unwanted tears now burned my cheeks; I tried to control them but could not. "I was so worried about her . . . and one word from you—*one word* and I wouldn't have had to worry any more."

"There was more involved than you realized," he said abruptly. "A woman was murdered. It was a matter of life and death. All I wanted to do was to keep you out of it—"

"As if you cared!" The harsh words seemed to sear the air between us. I bent my head, turned aside to hide the humiliation of tears. "As if it mattered to you! There's no need to insult me by pretending any further—"

He said, interrupting, his voice hard and angry: "There was no pretense. And no insult. And it mattered more than anything else in the world."

I put my hands over my ears and shook my head as if I could shake his words away. My eyes were dim with pain. I didn't see him move until I felt his arms slip around me and his breath cool against my hot cheek.

"Claire—"

"Let me go!" I twisted away from him. The pain was so excruciating that I could no longer think clearly; my movements were instinctive. I ran from him, stumbling down the path to the road, and although I would have turned back in a flash if he had called my name he said nothing and I knew then that he was relieved to see me go.

I was so upset that I forgot the car. My eyes, blind with tears, never even saw it as I stumbled past. I went downhill, down the road without knowing or caring where I was going. All I was aware of was the blurred brilliant green of the beech trees overhead and the patterns of light made by the sun as its shafts pierced the leaves and slanted across the road.

After a while I stopped running and slowed to a walk. My breath was coming in short gasps and there was an ache in my side. I stopped, bent double to rid myself of the pain, and then because it was easier to sit down than to straighten my back and go on again, I collapsed on the bank of the road. I sat there for a long time. No one came. Nothing happened. Occasionally a bird sang and once far away I heard the faint hum of an airplane.

At last I thought: how absurd to be so upset over a man I met less than a week ago! How unnecessary! I had behaved like an infatuated adolescent, imagining myself in the midst of a whirlwind love affair. The excitement of traveling to strange countries combined with the strain of Gina's disappearance had made me momentarily lose touch with reality. However, now I could begin to act like a reasonable, rational adult once again. I could be critical once more, cool, dispassionate and practical. Love at first sight was for the magazines, or for people like Gina whose personalities acted as a magnet to the opposite sex. Fairytale romances were for those with their heads in the clouds. As for me, I had my feet firmly on the ground, and fairytales no longer appealed to me.

I stood up. My legs felt weak and unsteady but I set off walking again. I passed the gates of Holmbury House and presently found myself on an open stretch of hillside covered with ferns and heather. Before me, stretching mistily into the horizon was a sweeping view of fields, trees and the faint outline of hills in the distance. The sun shone. The countryside was beautiful. And because it was so beautiful I felt overwhelmingly aware of the stark ugliness of my grief. Tears sprang to my eyes again, and before I could stop myself I was crying, fumbling ineffectually for a handkerchief.

I sat down again by the roadside.

Perhaps it would be better if I admitted I was in love and stopped telling myself I was behaving like an adolescent. I found the handkerchief, blew my nose, pressed a hand to my aching forehead. I felt physically ill. Later, perhaps, I could chalk the entire episode up to experience and resume the comforting dullness of my normal life, but now I found it was impossible for me to be so detached.

The pain of loss was intolerable.

I thought of my lonely little apartment high above Manhattan, the evenings spent alone, the days exhausted trying to teach girls a subject most of them were not interested in learning. My safe, secure, peaceful life! I had never realized before how empty it had been.

I stood up desperately as the present reached out long fingers to taint the past and blur the future. It was as if I had no future, no past, as if my present were as fleeting and yet as horrifying as a nightmare from which there was no escape. I was nothing suddenly. I looked around wildly, praying that I would see someone I could speak to, someone whom I could use to regain my grip on reality and check the disintegration of my world, and as I glanced across the open hillside to the road below I saw a green convertible emerge into view and begin its toil up the road towards me.

I waited.

The car drew nearer. As it approached me I saw it lose speed and the next moment it had halted beside me and the driver was pulling down the window.

"Claire!" exclaimed Eric Jantzen in astonishment. "Well, this is certainly a surprise! What are you doing down here in Surrey?"

Since I had forgotten that Garth and Lilian were entertaining French clients at the cottage that weekend, I was almost as surprised to see him as he was to see me. Just as I was foggily trying to invent a reply he said anxiously: "Is something wrong?"

"No," I said. I couldn't think of anything else to say.

"You've still not heard from Gina?"

"I haven't seen her at all." That much was true.

He shook his head in sympathy. "You look tired," he said kindly. "Everything must be a great strain for you at present. Would you like some coffee, perhaps? Or some tea? I'm just on my way to Garth's cottage, which is very near here, and I'm sure he wouldn't mind if you dropped in for a while. My wife and Garth are entertaining French clients over the weekend, and on those occasions I usually spend the weekend at the cottage too. However, they won't be there yet—they had to go to the airport this morning to meet the plane from Paris. They will all drive down here after lunch."

I stared at him blankly. I must have looked mentally deficient. "Oh," I said at last.

This was hardly a sparkling reply, but it seemed to encourage him to reiterate his invitation. "Let me make you some coffee! Please—you look so tired! The cottage isn't far from here, less than a mile—"

I thought in panic: I can't see Garth again. I couldn't possibly face him a second time. And then in confusion: Garth's secretary told me Lilian came down to the cottage last night to prepare everything for the weekend. Garth must have come instead, and Lilian must have gone to the airport to meet the clients. But why doesn't Eric know this? Why does he expect them both to be at the airport?

"Thank you very much," I heard myself say falteringly, "but I don't think I feel like coffee just now." I felt suddenly possessed with a desire to escape, and as soon as the notion crossed my mind I remembered that I had arrived at Garth's house in a car and that there was no escape until I went back to get it. "I—I wonder," I said stammering, "—if you could give me a lift to the cottage? It seems—I mean, I think I've left my car there."

He looked at me first in bewilderment and then sharply in speculation. I sensed he wanted to know why I had been at the cottage and what had happened to reduce me to a state in which I was capable only of producing a series of curious remarks. "Why, of course!" he said with reserve, his eyes watchful. "Jump in!"

He leaned over and opened the door of the passenger seat for me. As the car moved on up the road he said to me with an attempt to recapture his air of joviality: "You really should tell me what's been happening, you know! You don't seem to be yourself at all. What's been going on at the cottage?"

"Nothing," I said. "I thought Gina might be there but I was wrong. I walked away from my car down the road wondering what I should do next. I'm feeling more and more distressed with every hour that passes."

"Why, yes," he murmured, his eyes on the road. "Yes, I can understand that. It must be most upsetting."

The car purred on up the hill. We passed the houses, passed the sign which pointed to Peaslake and moved on along the twisting road to the cottage.

"Do you have a key?" I said suddenly.

"Oh yes," he said. "We all have a key. Occasionally,

153

if Garth's abroad, he lends us the cottage for weekends. He and Lilian do a certain amount of business entertaining here as well. It's very useful to them."

I was just opening my mouth to tell him that Garth wasn't at the airport after all when we rounded the last bend and the cottage came into sight.

I gasped. The words died on my lips.

"What's the matter?" said Eric swiftly. "What is it?"

"I—thought my car had a flat tire," I said faintly. "But that was a trick of the light. There's nothing wrong."

But I was lying. The shock I had received was not on account of my car, which still stood beneath the trees, but because there was no longer any sign of the creamy white Jaguar.

Garth had vanished.

"Are you sure you won't stop for coffee?" said Eric again, parking his car where Garth had left the Jaguar earlier. "It wouldn't be any trouble at all."

I was too dazed to argue further. I found the idea of coffee more than welcome, and now that Garth had gone there was no reason for me to refuse to enter the cottage. "Well, perhaps I'll change my mind," I said awkwardly. "Thank you very much."

I began to wonder where Garth had gone. If he had returned to Holmbury village he would have passed me on the road. I decided that for some reason or other he had driven on over the hill to Peaslake—perhaps to buy extra food from the shops there. As we walked up to the front door and Eric produced a key I started to feel nervous in case Garth returned from Peaslake before I had finished my coffee and left the cottage.

"Come in," said Eric, opening the door and standing back to allow me to cross the threshold before him.

There was no hall. The front door opened into a long, light living room with picture windows which faced the view across the valley below. There was a staircase to my right, and on the left were two other doors which I guessed led into the kitchen and dining room.

"Nice, isn't it?" said Eric genially from behind me. He spoke with the satisfaction of an owner, not a mere guest. "It's very restful here after London."

The room was filled with antiques. I noticed the Regency chairs and couch, the long carved oak chest along one wall, the grandfather clock by the stairs.

"It *is* nice," I said absently. "What a pity the house is modern and not an old-fashioned cottage to go with the old-fashioned furniture."

"You say that because you're American," he said. "We Europeans have no fond illusions about little old-fashioned cottages with damp in the walls and woodworm in the roof and icy drafts from ill-fitting windows in the winter." He waved a hand vaguely towards the couch. "Sit down— make yourself at home. I'll get the coffee."

I sat down while he disappeared into the kitchen, but presently I stood up again and wandered over to the door next to the kitchen. As I had guessed earlier, it led into a dining room. There was a china closet full of beautiful English china, and opposite it a corner cupboard filled with the most elegant glasses I had ever seen. Unable to resist the temptation. I opened the cabinet and took out a glass. The stem was so slender that I thought it would break in my hands, and the rim of the glass was as thin as paper. An engraved design ran lightly round the delicate edge. Putting the glass back hastily before such fragile beauty could splinter into fragments in my hands, I closed the cupboard door and wandered back into the living room.

"Eric, is there a bathroom on this floor?"

"No," he called. "It's upstairs. Second door on the left."

I moved slowly up the stairs. I was thinking of Garth again, wondering what he was doing, when he would be back. I began to hurry automatically. I must not stay in the house more than ten minutes. Then I must leave, drive away in the car, never see the cottage again . . .

I reached the landing and found I could no longer remember Eric's directions to the bathroom. All the doors were closed. I stared at them absently for a moment. Second door on the right? No, he had said the left. The second door? The third door on the left? I wandered down the tiny passage, opened the door, and walked straight into a closet containing a bundle of old clothes. Checking an exclamation of annoyance I was just turning away when I realized that the bundle of old clothes on the floor was not quite that.

I stopped, looked again . . .

My scalp prickled. Horror made the breath freeze in my throat. For one long moment I stood stock still staring down at that dreadful heap on the floor, and then rapidly, hardly aware of what I was doing, I bent down, pulled aside the old coat on top of the pile and found myself inches from a woman's face distorted by violent death. At first I didn't recognize her, and then . . .

It was Lilian Jantzen.

9

It seemed that I stood there motionless for a long time with my mind paralyzed by fright, and then slowly, mechanically I closed the door and leaned against it. I wanted to move, but as in all the most appalling nightmares, the paralysis of shock made movement impossible. After a hiatus which may have lasted no longer than thirty seconds but which seemed to last at least thirty minutes, I managed to step across the passage and blunder into the room opposite. I found myself in the bedroom and facing a picture window much like the one in the living room directly below me. It was now raining outside. Snarls of water spat against the enormous windowpane and trickled impotently down the glass to the sill.

It was very quiet.

I thought: whoever killed Lilian killed Thérèse as well, and who else could have killed them other than Garth or Eric; Warren might just conceivably have killed Thérèse but he couldn't have killed Lilian. Lilian must have been killed either last night, if she really did come down to the cottage then to prepare for the weekend, or else earlier this morning, and Warren has been with me since yesterday evening . . . or did he slip out last night after I had gone to bed? But no, that was before we hired the car, and without transportation how could he have made his way out here? So either Garth or Eric killed Lilian. And either Garth or Eric killed Thérèse.

I was so stupefied with the enormity of the realization that for a moment my mind refused to go further. I kept saying to myself: either Garth or Eric killed Lilian; either Garth or Eric killed Thérèse, and yet the simple question: which one? was something my mind refused to phrase. But suddenly I remembered something. If Gina was staying at Garth's flat she could give him an alibi for the previous evening. He could not have killed Lilian this morning since the house had been empty on my first visit and the body was too stiff to allow for the possibility that Garth had killed her on his arrival less than two hours ago . . .

I had to speak to Gina. If she could tell me that Garth had spent the previous evening with her I would know for certain that he was innocent.

There was a phone extension next to the bed. After fumbling dizzily in my purse for the number I picked up the receiver with shaking fingers and dialed O for the operator.

The line purred three times. Then: "Operator," said a pleasant voice into my ear.

"I wonder if you can help me," I said in a low rapid voice. "I'm trying to get through to a London number—Mayfair 75432. Could you try it for me, please?"

"Mayfair 75432? One moment." The line clicked and she was gone.

I waited. And waited.

"Trying to connect you," said the voice.

I went on waiting. My heart was bumping painfully against my lungs. My palms were so damp that the receiver slipped and almost fell from my fingers.

"Trying to connect you," said the voice again.

It was not until then that I remembered the code Gina

and Garth had established with telephone calls.

"I'm sorry," said the operator kindly, "but there's no reply."

"Wait," I said unevenly. "Please ring twice, then hang up, then ring again. Please."

In Britain perhaps they are more accustomed to eccentrics than they are in America. I could just imagine the smart retort I would have received from a New York operator if I had made the same request.

"One moment, please," said the voice placidly, and I heard her begin to dial again.

Maybe my request had provided her with an interesting variation in routine. I heard the bell ring twice at the other end of the wire, then a silence. Finally the bell began to ring again, but Gina hardly waited for it to ring once. There was a click as she picked up the receiver.

"Hello?"

"Go ahead, caller—"

"Gina, it's me. Listen, I can't talk. Just tell me one thing. Where was Garth last night?"

"Garth?" said Gina puzzled. "Last night? Why, he was here! He bought some groceries and I fixed him dinner. He was tired and went to bed early. Why?"

"Get off the line," I said rapidly. "Call the police. Lilian Jantzen's been murdered and her body is hidden in Garth's cottage. Get the police at once."

I heard her gasp. "I'll call them right away," she said and hung up.

I listened to the empty line for a second longer, too mesmerized by my knowledge even to replace the receiver in its cradle. Garth was innocent. And downstairs, alone with me in the house—

From somewhere far away on the dead line I heard a low stealthy click.

I froze.

Eric Jantzen had been listening in downstairs on the living room phone.

The receiver fell out of my hands and clattered on to the table. I could not breathe, speak or move. And then as I stood there in a paralysis of panic I heard his soft measured footsteps coming slowly up the stairs towards me.

I managed to move. I crossed the room, my feet making no noise on the thick carpet, and opened the door. He was at the top of the stairs. When I came out into the passage he stopped. We faced each other.

I thought: if I could edge towards the bathroom, I could lock myself in . . .

But he moved forward towards me and I stepped back into the bedroom.

"Rather rash of you, wasn't it?" he said, still determined to sound jovial. His little eyes, narrow above his fleshy cheeks, were empty of expression. He moved like an automaton, steadily, with precision.

I backed away until I was against the picture window and could retreat no more.

He stopped. "The police will arrest Garth," he said. "You must realize that. All the evidence points towards Garth."

"Yes," I said. Garth must come back soon from his expedition to Peaslake. I had an advantage in that I knew Garth was nearby while Eric thought he was still in London. If I could keep Eric talking until Garth arrived—

"But you don't believe Garth killed Lilian, do you?" he said. "That's why you phoned your sister. She was able to give him an alibi."

I said, playing for time, "The alibi was for last night. He could have killed her this morning."

"And the police will find out she wasn't killed this morning," he said. "I killed her last night, here at the cottage."

There was a silence. After a while I managed to say: "I don't understand."

"I was justified in killing her," he said as if this explained everything. "It was no more than she deserved. She was a murderess."

I stared at him. He found a handkerchief, mopped his face, and I saw for the first time that he was profoundly moved.

"She killed Thérèse," he said. "My wife killed another woman. My wife. Lilian. She was a cheat and a fraud and a murderess."

He was crying openly now. As I watched him with mingled horror and pity, he twisted his handkerchief in his hands. Presently when he was able to speak again he said: "Lilian said it was an accident that Thérèse died, but I don't think it was. I think she meant to kill her. Thérèse knew vital—damaging facts—"

"About Lilian."

"About Lilian. Lilian had swindled Garth out of ten thousand pounds last year by pretending the company owed more to the Inland Revenue than it actually did. Lilian did the books, filed the tax returns; two years ago she had got into debt by trying to expand the business still further, handling contracts which were a little too big to handle. Money was lost, and the profits were low that year. But she had expected the profits to be higher and she had already spent her share . . . she needed money, and as time passed the need for money became pressing. So she cheated. She took money which should have been split between herself and Garth. She could have taken out a loan—borrowed the money—something—but no, she had to cheat. 'If I borrowed there would be so much money wasted in interest,' she said. 'Money that could be put into the business.' She was quite ruthless where the business was concerned. She wouldn't listen to reason. 'Garth will never know,' she said. 'He always leaves the books to me. He'll never find out.' So she took the money and cheated him and laid herself open to blackmail."

After a moment I said: "But how did Thérèse know that Lilian had cheated Garth?"

"I told her," he said simply.

There was a silence. Everything was very still.

"It was like this," he said suddenly. "Thérèse was an ally, a friend. She wanted to break up any attachment existing between Garth and Lilian as much as I did, and she was convinced that an attachment existed. Three months ago she followed them when they went to a conference in Paris—they were both staying at Garth's *pied à-terre* . . . well, we needn't go into that. Thérèse saw me afterwards and expected me to make some sort of scene with Lilian. She didn't know that Lilian wouldn't have cared if I had. Lilian wanted to leave me. She's had no use for me for some time."

Tears furrowed his face again, and the rain wept with him, hurling itself against the windowpane.

"But I loved her," he said. "I was prepared to do anything to prevent her from leaving. When Thérèse asked me why I would not fight with Lilian over the episode with Garth in Paris, I told her the truth—that Lilian would have welcomed the chance to be rid of me and that to make a scene would have been pointless. I told Thérèse that the only reason I managed to keep

Lilian living under the same roof with me was because I knew she had cheated Garth and I threatened to tell him so unless she stayed with me as my wife."

"What did Thérèse say?"

"Nothing—then. Oh, she probably had a row with Garth but she didn't approach Lilian. That came later." He stopped. "Last Saturday," he said painfully. "Less than a week ago. Last Saturday she stormed into our flat when I was out and Lilian was there alone, and told Lilian that she would make trouble for her unless she left Garth alone. She had had a row with Garth earlier, she said. She told Lilian that Garth was pretending to be interested in a young American girl who had arrived with him the previous evening from Paris, but that she herself wasn't deceived for a moment; Garth's interest in Gina was merely a smokescreen to conceal his interest in Lilian. Thérèse told me the same thing when I had seen her the previous evening; after she had met Garth and Gina at London airport she phoned and asked to see me, and when I met her she told me exactly what was on her mind. And I agreed with her. Gina wasn't Garth's type. I too believed that he was merely using her as a smokescreen.

"I saw Thérèse on Friday night. Early Saturday evening she had a showdown with Garth at her flat and then, still not satisfied, she came to our flat and saw Lilian herself. It was then that she told Lilian that unless she kept her hands off Garth, Thérèse would tell both Garth and the Fraud Squad that Lilian had cheated him out of a considerable sum of money. It was the worst thing she could possibly have said. Lilian lived for her business—it was husband, child, lover, everything to her. She had started it, built it up, nurtured it to success. Where the business was concerned she was fanatical—irrational. She

163

would do anything to protect it. And then along came
Thérèse talking of the Fraud Squad, criminal proceedings
the business's reputation smeared beyond repair. . . .

"I don't know what happened next. Lilian said she
and Thérèse came to blows and Thérèse accidentall
slipped and struck her head and died. But I don't thin
the death was so accidental as that. I think Lilian delib
erately killed her. . . . But there was Thérèse—dead—
killed either by accident or design—and in our flat!

"When I came in half an hour afterwards Lilian ha
dragged the body to the spare bedroom and locked th
door. She was more distraught than I had ever seen he
look before. She told me what had happened and said
must help her, and it was then suddenly that I saw wha
I could do; I promised to help her get rid of the body i
she would agree to give our marriage a completely nev
start, never see Garth except at the office and allow m
to come with her on all her business trips with him.

"She said she would. She promised. She swore she
would do everything I said. So I went out again, to
place I knew down by the river in Pimlico where they
sell second-hand trunks and suitcases. Lilian said she
must establish an alibi—she rang up a friend, suggeste
they go to the cinema together. I left her while she wa
still talking on the phone . . . I had completely forgotte
that a few hours before, at lunch, I had invited Gina t
call at the flat for a drink that evening. The thought o
Gina never even crossed my mind.

"I couldn't find a trunk at that hour—all the shop
were shut, even the one I had thought of in Pimlico, an
so I decided I would have to use one of Lilian's larg
suitcases instead. I went back to the flat, and not realizin
that Lilian had already left for the cinema, I called ou
to tell her that I hadn't been able to find a trunk fo

the body and that we'd have to use a large suitcase. When there was no reply I realized she had left. I set to work at once, found the suitcase, managed to shut the lid with the body inside. Then when everything was ready I took the case out to the car and drove down to Holmbury St. Mary. I thought that if I buried the body in the garden of the cottage no one would come across it, and if the grave was discovered, they would suspect Garth and not us. Garth never bothered with the garden, although sometimes he talked vaguely of hiring a gardener—I thought there was a good chance he wouldn't stroll to the bottom of the garden till the weeds had grown over the grave again.

"When everything was finished at the cottage I went back to London to the flat. Lilian had returned from the cinema and was waiting for me. She said: 'How did you get rid of Gina when you got back from Pimlico?' I didn't know what she meant. And then I remembered that I had told Gina to come by for a drink. 'I let her in,' Lilian said. 'Didn't she wait for you to come back?' And I realized that Gina might have been there when I called out to Lilian to tell her I couldn't find a trunk for the body—she might have been hiding nearby when I had put the body in the suitcase. We talked it over, Lilian and I. It was possible Gina hadn't bothered to wait for me and had left before I returned, but we had to make sure. We tried to find her—and couldn't. She had disappeared. Vanished. There was no trace of her."

"Garth was hiding her," I said shakily. "I found that out today."

"Garth's a clever actor. He had us both convinced he hadn't set eyes on the girl since last Saturday, when we all had lunch together. At least he had me convinced. Lilian . . ." He broke off, staring into nothingness, his mind abstracted and remote from me.

I hardly dared breathe for fear of interrupting hi[s] train of thought and reminding him of my existence i[n] the room. I wanted to ask why he had killed Lilian but let the silence linger on unbroken as the rain swept acros[s] the hillside from the valley below.

"The police came later," he said after a while. "W[e] heard then about the hysterical phone call Gina had mad[e] to you. The police found nothing at the flat, but we kne[w] then that we had to find Gina somehow. She was dangerous to us. We wondered if she would go to the police bu[t] Lilian thought not. The police might have thought Gin[a] and Thérèse had quarreled over Garth and Gina woul[d] be a chief suspect if inquiries were made into Thérèse['s] murder."

I waited, my body aching with tension, and as [I] watched him he raised his eyes slowly and looked at me. I said quickly, seizing the first subject which came t[o] mind: "I don't understand why Lilian died."

"Because she broke her word," he said. "After all [I] did for her—after I had disposed of the body and managed to conceal her crime—after all that she broke he[r] promise. She promised she would give up Garth altogether and give our marriage a fresh start, but she didn'[t] mean it. This so-called 'business weekend' here at th[e] cottage was fictitious—there were no clients expected t[o] arrive in London on the Friday morning plane. I had [a] hunch she was lying to me and I called Rémy International in France to check whether the two men were du[e] in England this weekend. I was told that they weren't. A[s] soon as I found this out last night I drove down here t[o] the cottage—Lilian had arrived here earlier, supposedl[y] to prepare everything for the visitors. When I got her[e] she pretended to be astonished—she denied everything—

said I was out of my mind. . . ." He stopped. Then: "Out of my mind," he repeated, as if amazed by his own choice of phrase. "She said I was out of my mind . . . I told her I knew very well she had merely planned a weekend with Garth, but she wouldn't admit it. She went on lying—on and on. . . . And then suddenly there were no more lies, only silence. It was a terrible blank silence. Afterwards I was so upset that I panicked and rushed away back to London—I only stopped long enough to push the body in the cupboard and then I drove and drove all along those twisting country roads. It was all so dark and still and silent. . . .

"This morning I managed to pull myself together. I knew I must drive down again to the cottage and bury the body. I must pretend to be normal, act as though nothing had happened. That was why when I stopped to talk to you I invited you here for coffee—I was so anxious to appear normal, as if nothing was wrong. But why did *you* come down here? Why were you so shaken? I seemed to sense you suspected me. When you made the excuse to go upstairs I thought: supposing she wanted the excuse to search the house? And you were gone such a long time. . . . Then I heard the faint ring the phone makes whenever the extension in the bedroom is used, and I knew what must have happened."

"I wanted to ask my sister where Garth was last night."

"But why should she have known? Where was Garth hiding her anyway?"

"In his apartment," I said.

He stared at me. "She had been with him in his apartment all this week?"

In a flash I saw how I could catch him off balance. "Why do you think Gina came to London with him from Paris?" I said. "Gina was infatuated with him. You were wrong in suspecting your wife was involved. It was Gina, not Lilian who was infatuated."

He went on staring at me. "But this business weekend which proved to be non-existent—"

"Rémy International must have misinformed you. Garth's secretary confirmed the appointment when I spoke to her earlier today."

After a long silence he whispered: "I don't believe it."

"Well, you didn't believe Lilian," I said, "so there's no reason why you should believe me. But I think Lilian was telling the truth. Besides, I don't think Garth would have been interested in an illicit weekend with her. He had other fish to fry."

"I don't believe it," he repeated. "I don't believe it." He was very white. I saw him begin to tremble as he half turned away from me, and then he was struck dumb as he began to realize what I was suggesting . . . he had killed his wife for an infidelity which had existed only in his imagination.

I moved. I darted across the room, tried to push past him into the passage beyond, but he caught me by the wrist, jerked me back into the room. I struggled wildly but he was much too strong for me, and although I screamed and screamed for help no one came.

I was powerless, frantic with terror. I tried to scream again in one last desperate burst of strength but his fingers closed around my throat and the scream died on my lips. The room tilted, swirled before my eyes, and as the blood started to sing in my ears I knew dimly that all was lost and that there was nothing more I could do.

10

The pressure eased very suddenly. There was a roaring in my ears but gradually that too ceased. I found I could see again. I was on the floor, the carpet grazing my knuckles, and as I struggled to my feet I saw Eric was standing a few feet away from me, his eyes staring at the doorway.

I turned my head slowly, frowning at the pain, my mind clouded with shock, my whole being numbed with incomprehension, and found myself looking at a black, ugly automatic. The automatic was held by a strong firm hand and looked as if it were comfortably at home there.

"Are you all right, Claire?" It was Garth's voice.

It was too painful to nod and my own voice seemed to have disappeared. I managed to stand up but immediately sat down again on the edge of the bed.

"Did he hurt you?"

"Well, of course he hurt me!" Shock made me unreasonably angry. "Where the hell were you? Why did you go away? I was nearly killed!"

"Whose idea was it for you to come back here?" he asked mildly. "Not mine! God Almighty, you almost *were* murdered!" He swung back to Eric. "We'll go downstairs. You can lead the way. Clasp your hands behind your head. I don't want to have any accidents in transit."

Eric moved blindly out into the passage.

"Come on, Claire."

"Don't you order me about!" I stormed. And then, stammering: "I—I'm sorry—I'm not myself—"

"I understand." He waited for me by the doorway, his eyes still watching the other man, but when I reached him, he took my hand in his and held it for a moment. "All right, Eric. Move on."

It was then I saw that the door of the adjacent room was open and what looked like a portable tape recorder playing silently just beyond the threshold.

"Switch that off, would you, Claire? Just pull the plug out of the wall but don't touch the machine."

I mechanically did as I was told. My mind refused even to try to reconstruct what had happened, but I was dimly aware that Garth must have somehow managed to record most, if not all, of my conversation with Eric in the bedroom. We went downstairs.

"Stand right there, Eric, and don't move. You can put your hands down. Claire, I'd advise you to have a shot of brandy. There's a bottle under the sideboard over there and a glass in the dining room."

He went to the phone, the gun still in his right hand, and removed the receiver with his left. Putting down the receiver on the table he began to dial, still using his left hand.

He dialed nine-nine-nine.

"Police, please." He saw me still standing motionless by the dining room door. "Please, Claire—get the brandy and sit down! You look—hello? Police? My name is Cooper and I'm speaking from Coneyhurst Cottage on Holmbury Hill—it's the last cottage before Peaslake on the Holmbury-Peaslake road. Could you come over here at once, please? A woman's been murdered."

I went into the dining room in a daze and tried to find

a glass which I wouldn't be afraid of breaking but all the glasses were the fragile collector's items which I had noticed earlier; my fingers were still so unsteady that I was convinced I would drop any glass I touched, so at last in despair I went to the kitchen and took a cup from the cupboard.

Garth had just hung up when I emerged into the living room once more with the cup in my hand. "Good God, you can't drink Courvoisier out of a teacup!"

"It's a receptacle, isn't it?" I said doggedly. "What can prevent me drinking out of it if I want to?"

It showed the measure of our shock that we were so ready to argue over trivialities.

Eric said he wanted to sit down.

"All right. Take that chair over there."

"I'd like a drink too," he added.

Garth motioned me to pour one for him. Then he said harshly: "How can you be so calm, Eric? If I hadn't been in the house you would have killed Claire, too."

"No . . . no, it was just that I—I suddenly saw—realized—"

"That I wasn't and never had been interested in having an affair with your cold, clever, crooked wife? That you had killed her for nothing?"

Eric said stumbling: "It was such a shock . . . I was overcome . . . I wanted to kill her for telling me, showing me the truth—"

"If you had had an ounce of sense you'd never have listened to Thérèse. Good God, you could have had your wife and good luck to you! Couldn't you guess I could hardly wait to get enough capital behind me to work my way out of the partnership? Did you ever really think I was the kind of man who enjoyed answering to a woman and being told by her what to do the whole damned time? Lilian was still the boss, you know, even though we were officially partners. It was she who had picked me out from the obscure ranks of all the salesmen in London and selected me to work for her—and, my God, she never let me forget it! I was grateful to her and glad of the opportunities she gave me but I got pretty damned tired of playing second fiddle day in, day out, year after year—"

"Then why did you stay with her?"

"I very nearly didn't! We had our quarrels and disagreements, but I knew I could never make so much money so quickly elsewhere and I wanted more than anything else to amass capital, be independent. But unlike you I don't expect my wife to support me while I indulge in unprofitable speculation. When I marry we'll live on my money, not on my wife's."

"Lilian understood—"

"She understood nothing but the business! And cared for nothing but the business! And you know that as well as I do. Just because you had the misfortune to be in love with her, don't make the mistake of assuming she also knew what love meant. Maybe she did once, long ago, when you first knew her, but certainly I never once caught a glimpse of understanding in her. She wasn't interested in love! She didn't care—not for you, not for anyone. She was narrow-minded and cold and utterly selfish. If you hadn't been so unbalanced as to try and strangle Claire just now I'd feel you were justified in murdering Lilian, and I wouldn't be aiming this gun at you at all."

"I didn't mean to harm Claire—I was overwhelmed—dazed—"

"You did mean to harm her. You put your hands deliberately round her throat and equally deliberately

172

tried to throttle her into unconsciousness."

"I didn't know what I was doing—"

"Tell that to the police, not to me. I might become 'overwhelmed' and 'dazed' too and feel an uncontrollable urge to pull the trigger."

There was heavy silence. At last Garth said to me: "How are you feeling now?"

"Better." I gripped the cup tightly but my fingers were still trembling. "Where did you go after I left here?"

"Nowhere. I drove the car up to the top of the hill and hid it in the bushes. Then I walked back and prepared to set up my tape recorder. I'd found Lilian dead when I arrived earlier, but since I was still expecting Eric to turn up I went ahead with my plans to tape a confession. Unfortunately I set the machine up in the living room, which was no use at all when you both moved upstairs to the bedroom. I was forced to come out of the cupboard under the stairs where I'd been hiding and follow you upstairs, tape recorder and all. Fortunately it was reasonably portable.

"I'd been working towards it all week. Eric was right in believing that the business weekend was a fiction, but wrong in assuming Lilian knew it was fictitious. She didn't know. I planned to have a showdown with both the Jantzens, since I believed they were both involved in Thérèse's murder, so I invented the visit of the representatives of Rémy International and paved the way for luring both of them here to the cottage where Thérèse was buried. I reasoned they would be more likely to be trapped into an admission out here in a remote spot, with Thérèse's grave only a few yards away at the end of the garden."

"No wonder you were so anxious to get rid of me this morning!"

"Yes, I'd just found Lilian's body and was trying to work out what I should do next; for all I knew Eric would arrive any minute—I'm sorry if I was too abrupt but I was worried in case things went wrong. I'd taken a gamble in not going to the police. When I heard that Thérèse was dead and that Eric had taken the body out of the flat to dispose of it, I knew immediately that when the body was found I'd be the number one. And if the police believed that Gina and I were involved with one another, Gina would be suspect number two. Thérèse was jealous, quite capable of initiating disastrous scenes it was Gina and I who would immediately come under suspicion if she were killed, not the Jantzens, who had no such obvious motive for murdering her. I had a key to the Jantzen apartment and no alibi for Saturday night—to the police that would all add up to motive, means, and opportunity for committing the crime. The same applied to Gina—she was actually there on the scene of the murder, and her presence could be proved by the phone call she made to New York and your report of the call to Scotland Yard."

"What did Gina do after she had phoned me that evening? And why did she hang up so suddenly?"

"She thought she heard the front door opening, but it was a false alarm—a noise from the flat below. By the time she realized this she'd already replaced the receiver and cut off the call. She pulled herself together and saw she had to get out of the flat at once—she told me she'd panicked as soon as Eric left with the body, and made the call to you without even pausing to think what she was doing."

"Yes," I said shakily. "That sounds like Gina."

"However, after cutting herself off from you she left the flat, found the nearest callbox and dialed my number.

I was the only other person she knew in London. I told her to come over to my flat at once, and she did. We reasoned that the Jantzens would work out that she had seen too much, so I decided she must lie low and communicate with nobody. Early the next morning I drove her down here, as I knew the Jantzens intended to be in town all week."

Eric said unexpectedly: "But we checked the cottage! On Monday I drove down here—"

"Gina had left by then—fortunately. Later on Sunday evening she discovered Thérèse's body, just as Claire did this morning. This so unnerved her that she immediately called a taxi and left for Dorking, where she put up at a hotel. She tried to contact me but by that time I'd left for Paris—I had to go for unavoidable business reasons, and besides I was anxious to act normally, as if nothing had happened. Gina nearly wrote to me in Paris but remembered I was returning to London on Wednesday morning and that a letter to Paris might miss me. So she wrote to my home address in London in order that, as soon as I reached home, I would know where she was and where I could contact her. When I heard what had happened I told her to come to my flat in London. I didn't think it was safe for her to stay anywhere else. On my return I began to set the scene for a showdown at the cottage; I knew by then where Thérèse's body was and I thought I could see a way to establish our innocence and prove the Jantzens' guilt."

"How did you find Lilian's body this morning?" I asked.

"I was puzzled because she wasn't here to meet me—we had arranged that she was to come down here last night to get the place ready, and when I arrived I intended to tell her that Rémy International had postponed the

175

visit at the last minute, and to suggest she and Eric have lunch here with me before driving back to town. As soon as Eric arrived I was going to launch into my counsel for the prosecution act for the benefit of the tape recorder. Having planned everything so carefully it gave me a shock to find Lilian wasn't here when I arrived. On an impulse I decided to search the house, and a couple of minutes later I opened the door of the cupboard upstairs and found her."

In the armchair by the fireplace Eric moved. I started nervously, but for nothing. He had merely leaned forward and buried his face in his hands, as if the mention of Lilian's name and the manner of her death were sufficient to remove him from us, a human being cut off and isolated by grief and despair.

I wondered how long the police would take to arrive. Surely by now they must be well on their way! My fingers fidgeted endlessly with the cup in my hands and as I glanced at Eric again I saw him start and look up abruptly.

"What's that noise?"

Garth didn't move. "What noise?"

"I thought I heard a noise in the kitchen—"

"Stay where you are!" Garth had the gun trained on him. His back was to the kitchen door. "You needn't think you can fool me with that kind of trick."

But I was taut once more with nervousness, every muscle in my body aching with tension. I turned to face the kitchen door, the cup slipping in my clammy hands, and to my horror I saw the handle begin to turn.

I screamed.

Garth swung round but he wasn't quick enough. The door was already wide open.

"All right, Cooper," said a cool, tough voice I barely

recognized. "Put down that gun."

I stared incredulously, unable to believe what I saw, and found myself face to face with Warren Mayne.

It all happened so quickly that now as I look back I find it hard to recall the scene in any clear detail. I remember crying out something to Warren; I remember Garth, caught off balance, lowering his gun for a moment—and then in a flash, Eric was upon him and they were fighting for the weapon.

Warren shouted something, but neither of them paid him any attention.

"Help him—separate them—" I scarcely knew what I was saying. I darted forward, but before I could reach Garth, Warren said sharply: "Keep back, Claire. Cooper, drop that gun, or I'll—"

"No—no—" My voice rang high-pitched and terrified in my ears.

Garth slipped on the carpet, fell sideways against the table. The gun jerked out of his hand, spun in the air and thudded dully upon the carpet six inches from Eric's right hand.

For the last time that day, I heard myself scream.

"Right," said Warren busily, moving in as Eric seized the gun. "Now then—"

There was a deafening explosion as Eric pulled the trigger. I smelt acrid smoke, glimpsed the horrified expression on Warren's face, and then just before I fainted I saw the gun fall from Eric's hand and the blood run from his mouth as he lay dying.

11

When I regained consciousness the room was full of
policemen and Eric's body was covered with a sheet so
that I could no longer see his face. Warren, white and
stupefied, was saying helplessly to no one in particular:
"But I don't understand. I thought . . ." But he could
not even bring himself to say what he had thought. My
head ached, my mouth was dry, and someone was hold-
ing me in his arms as if I were a fragile piece of bone
china. I stirred, turned fuzzily towards him. I was lying
on the Regency couch and my head was propped against
his chest.

"Here," he said, "Drink this."

Brandy burned my throat again. My brain stirred and
I felt more capable of physical movement, A police
inspector, seeing that I was conscious, came over and
asked me kindly how I felt.

"Almost all right, thank you," I said with an effort.

"Good. We'll take a statement from you just as soon as
possible and then someone can drive you back home
Now, who did the suicide weapon belong to? Was it
yours, Mr. Cooper?"

"Yes, it was."

"May I see your license for it, please? Just a formality
you understand."

"Yes." He rose to his feet, placed some cushions gently

under my head and stooped to see that I was comfortable. Our glances met. I smiled shakily, and felt better.

"Now, young man," the inspector was saying paternally to Warren. "I noted you were carrying a gun too. Do you have a license?"

"Well . . . no," said Warren confused, "It's not an English gun. I bought it in Paris. I'm an American citizen."

"Dear me," said the inspector mildly. "Quite an international history. Thank you, Mr. Cooper," he added, glancing at Garth's license and giving it back to him. "Now I think we'll take a few statements. Supposing we start with you, Miss Sullivan—if you're well enough, of course."

I said I was. We went into the dining room and the inspector and I sat down at the table, while a sergeant sat on a chair in the corner with a pencil and notebook. Under the inspector's direction I told my story from start to finish, beginning with Gina's phone call to me the previous Saturday. The inspector listened and nodded sympathetically, for all the world as if he were a family doctor chatting with an old friend who sought advice. In the corner, the sergeant's pencil whispered steadily across the pages of his notebook.

At last, when I had finished and there was nothing left to tell, the inspector thanked me and said he would have one of his men drive me back to the hotel in Dorking.

"I—I'd rather wait for Mr. Cooper," I said awkwardly. "Is it all right if I stay here?"

"Mr. Cooper may be rather a long time, so I wouldn't advise you to wait. If I were you I'd go back to the hotel and rest for a while. Maybe you'd like Mr. Mayne to drive you back? I doubt if we need keep him long."

I had insufficient strength for an argument so I gave in meekly.

"And you'll keep in touch with us, please, if you don't mind," said the inspector cosily. "We'll want you to sign your statement when it's been typed and you've had a chance to read it over."

"Yes," I said. "Yes, of course."

In the living room, someone was taking photographs of the body. More police appeared to have arrived. The house was overflowing with dark blue uniforms. The inspector asked Warren to step into the dining room and as he obeyed uneasily, I looked around for Garth but there was no sign of him. Wandering into the kitchen I looked out of the window and saw him with three policemen at the bottom of the garden by Thérèse's grave.

I sat down on the couch again to wait. After about ten minutes Garth came back into the living room and moved swiftly across the room towards me.

"Is everything all right? Is someone going to drive you back to Dorking?" He glanced with distaste at the body still waiting for the ambulance, as if it were wrong for me to be in the same room as such a macabre object. "I'd drive you back myself but I can't leave till I've given a statement to the police."

"I think Warren will drive me back. The inspector offered to get one of his men to chauffeur us but I said I'd wait." Because I wanted to talk to you, I might have added, but there was no time; Warren chose that moment to emerge from the dining room. He looked older, graver and more careworn than I had ever seen him look before.

"I want to apologize," he said, walking right up to Garth and planting himself on the carpet before him. "I just don't know how to say it. If Jantzen hadn't turned that gun on himself—"

"Quite," said Garth, embarrassed by this naked display of emotion, even though the display was made with obvious sincerity. "But he did. Forget it—it's all over now."

"Yes, but if I hadn't been such a fool and messed everything up—"

"Could you take Claire back to Dorking, please? She's had a tough day and I don't think she should be here a moment longer." He turned towards me; there was an expression in his eyes which made my heart turn over. "I'll be in touch with you."

"Yes—all right, Garth."

"And don't dare jump on the night flight to America."

"No, Garth."

"If you do, I'll be following you on the morning plane."

I could not speak, but managed to smile. There were tears in my eyes. Everything seemed to shine and glitter hazily in the dim artificial light from the ceiling above us.

"Mr. Cooper?" said the inspector's voice politely from behind us. "Perhaps we could take your statement now, sir."

"Yes," said Garth. "Yes, of course."

"Come on, Claire." Warren's hand was on my arm. "Let's get away from here."

I followed him slowly out of the cottage. It was late afternoon, but still raining so hard that it was already twilight. The rain felt cool and refreshing against my cheek.

Warren led the way over to a small blue car which was unfamiliar to me.

"But this isn't the car I came in," I said stupidly.

"No, we'll have the car agency people pick up that one later. This is the car I hired to drive out here after you." He helped me get in, shut the door and went around to the other side to slide into the driver's seat.

"But I told you I'd spoken to Gina in Garth's office," I said, memory returning. "You were all set to go to London. Why didn't you go?"

"I figured you weren't being quite on the level with me." He switched on the engine. "You were acting too oddly and looked too shook up. After you'd left me to go to rest in your room, I called Garth's office to check to see if Gina had been there, and the secretary thought I was some kind of nut. So I went to your room and got no answer when I knocked on the door. That was when I got convinced you hadn't been on the level with me. When I went out into the courtyard and found the car gone it didn't take much brainwork to figure you'd gone off somewhere on your own, and where else would you go but to the cottage? After a bit of difficulty I managed to hire another car and come right on here after you. I couldn't think what you were playing at but I thought it wouldn't do any harm to find out."

"I should have trusted you," I said ashamed. "But the evidence was all against Garth and somehow I wanted to prove to myself that he was innocent before I told you what I'd discovered." I began to tell him how I had found Thérèse's body in its shallow grave, returned much shaken to Dorking, and tried to telephone Garth only to have my call answered by Gina herself. "She told me to join her at once in London," I said. "But I was too stupid to follow her advice. I felt I had to try and see Garth at the cottage and find out what was going on."

"I can't imagine why you were so convinced Garth was innocent," said Warren, interested. "Was that feminine intuition, would you say?"

"Yes," I said wryly. "I guess you could call it that."

We were freewheeling gently down the narrow twisting

road and had just passed the spot where I had met Eric earlier. I glanced out across the beautiful view again, but the rain made the landscape misty and the light was too obscure to enable me to see far. "He seems to like you," Warren ventured delicately, after a pause.

"Yes," I admitted.

"I guess he wouldn't have said that bit about following you to America if he'd been interested in Gina."

"I guess not." So that was his point!

"Maybe there never was anything much between him and Gina. Maybe I just read too much into their relationship. Maybe it was all pretty casual after all."

"Maybe."

This seemed to cheer him up. His new, older, more careworn expression lasted until we reached the junction with the main road at Abinger Hammer, and then he hummed gently under his breath all the way to Dorking.

The mist and early darkness made the town look mysterious and ghostly and very old. Not even the twentieth-century traffic could detract from West Street's antiquity, the ancient houses, the little pub built centuries ago, the glimpse of cobbled side streets. We reached the High Street, crawled past modern shops and returned to antiquity as we drove under the arch of the inn and into the courtyard beyond.

"Let's see if we can get something to eat," Warren said. "We're too early for dinner but maybe they have tea."

"I'd like some coffee."

We entered the hotel and wandered through the lounge towards the reception desk. Someone was checking in, someone tall and willowy with familiar blonde hair straying from underneath a preposterous hat. She wore an incredibly ugly coat, macabre stockings and flat-heeled shoes, and still managed to look beautiful.

183

Parisian perfume wafted delicately across the lobby towards us.

Warren and I simultaneously opened our mouths, bu she turned before we could speak and smiled her radiant dazzling smile as she caught sight of us.

"Darlings!" she exclaimed tremulously. "How utterly wonderful to see you both again! I'm *so* sorry you've had such trouble finding me . . ."

"You won't believe it," said Gina, "but none of thi would have happened if I hadn't been so inquisitive. Yo remember Miss Stick, our old Sunday school teacher back home? She always used to tell Mother that my curiosity would be my undoing, and she was so right. It was."

It was an hour later. After our confused, disjointe reunion in the lobby of the hotel, and my discovery tha when the inspector had been interviewing me Garth ha called Gina to tell her it was safe for her to come out o hiding, we had spent some time talking in one of th lounges before I had excused myself to go upstairs t my room. Gina had followed me ten minutes later an was now reclining gracefully on the end of my bed whil I, propped up against the pillows, had slipped back int my rôle of guide, philosopher and friend.

"You mean," I said dryly, "that your curiosity wa the sole reason for your so-called undoing?"

"The sole reason," said Gina with conviction. "Hon estly. You see, there I was—in the Jantzen apartment o Saturday night and waiting for Eric to arrive to have drink with me as he'd promised, and to tell me all abou Dino di Lasci and the Italian film scene and all the res of it, and Lilian had just excused herself and rushed o somewhere, and there I was—all alone with nothing t do except to wonder what Garth's relationship wit

184

Lilian was (and you must admit, darling, it was rather *peculiar* to think of a man like Garth working with a woman on an earnest businesslike plane, especially as Lilian was rather attractive in a cosy maternal sort of way) and—" She lost her way in the labyrinthine sentence, drew a breath and started again. "So I thought I'd just have a tiny peep around the apartment. Not a big snoop or anything, but just a little peep—"

"What were you expecting to find?" I said with interest. "Love letters, half burned in the grate? Compromising photographs?"

"Well, not *exactly* . . . I'm not really sure what I expected to find, but I just thought it might be interesting and I had nothing else to do—"

"So you went and looked around and while you were out of sight Eric opened the front door and called out to Lilian that he hadn't been able to get a trunk for the body."

"So you know already," said Gina disappointed. "Yes, I guess you would by now. But darling, can you imagine! I was in the master bedroom, and after he said that, I couldn't even move, let alone speak. And when I thought he was going to come into the bedroom! I hid behind the door and watched through the crack, and he opened the door of the room opposite which must have been some kind of spare room and then I saw it—the body, I mean—and of course I recognized it at once because Thérèse had made an awful scene at the airport when Garth and I had arrived the night before. Well, naturally I was just stiff with fright. I couldn't do anything except watch. He got a suitcase out of the closet and—no, I can't even talk about it. It was so awful. Finally after hours and hours—minutes really, I guess—he went out with the suitcase and I was alone again. Then I kind of

185

went mad. I wanted to scream and couldn't. I nearly ran out of the apartment and then I thought that if he came back for something he'd forgotten we'd meet in the elevator, so I forced myself to stay in the apartment for a few minutes. But I was so terrified I felt I had to talk to someone—anyone—but preferably—"

"Me," I said.

"But Claire, you're always so marvelously cool and sane and well balanced—"

"So well balanced I shut my eyes and dived right in to share all the fun."

"Well, of course I was horrified when I tried to call you back later and found I couldn't get through. As I told you on the phone, I called back twice later on Saturday night from Garth's apartment and the line was busy each time—"

"I was calling Scotland Yard and having your call traced."

"I meant to call again on Sunday but Garth drove me down to the cottage to hide and I found the grave in the garden—heavens! I was in such a state after that that I couldn't even make a phone call. Finally on Monday I tried again—and got no reply—"

"I was en route to Paris by then."

"Then Garth said he'd found you in Paris! Honestly, Claire, I could have wept. When I thought of all that money you must have spent—on a wild goose chase! And all because I'd been so selfish and dragged you in without even *thinking*—"

"All's well that ends well," I said mundanely. "At least I had a trip to Europe."

"I don't think all's well that ends well at all," Gina objected. "You won't be able to buy your little red car—"

I remembered vaguely that at one time the idea of

possessing a car had seemed important.

"—I missed several important modeling dates. Warren has probably lost his job by taking off without proper permission to come and look for me. . . . By the way, wasn't it sweet of him to go to all that trouble? There's something terribly *comforting* about Warren. When he says he'll move heaven and earth you know he probably will—you know he's not just saying it to sound impressive. When I saw him with you in the lobby I felt a lump in my throat. After all, it's marvelous to know someone cares *that* much."

"Hm," I said.

"And you know, Claire, to be absolutely honest and frank with you and to tell the complete truth—"

"Please do."

"I was a little disappointed in Garth. He was *so* glamorous in Paris! Yet when I was forced to share his apartment with him I found I was bored. Isn't that terrible? But it was true. I thought it would be so romantic to have him hiding me and to be forced to live at close quarters with him for a few days, but the odd thing was that he seemed to lose all interest in romance. Of course, I realize he had a lot on his mind, but . . . well, never mind. But even when he was at home and resting he just liked to read and listen to Beethoven quartets or something. There wasn't even a television. I did my best not to be a nuisance—I fixed him meals and cleaned every room until it looked like something out of an advertisement, but . . . well, nothing happened. I'm sure if it had been Warren—"

"Yes," I said. "Warren's much more suitable for you."

"You told me all along I should marry him, didn't you?"

"I do remember mentioning it now and then—"

"I think I will. I feel after all this that I just want to settle down and be an ordinary housewife and have six children."

"Wait till that feeling's passed," I couldn't help saying anxiously, "and then see if you still want to marry him. After all—"

There was a knock on the door. Gina swept across the room to answer it.

"Warren!"

"Gina!"

They faced each other starry-eyed. I swung my legs off the bed and went over to study the view from the window. Outside it was dark and still raining and the town lights were blurred as I stared out into the night.

"By the way, Warren," I said suddenly without turning to face him. "Why didn't you tell me you'd been in England last weekend?"

"Last weekend?" echoed Gina. "In England? Were you, Warren?"

I glanced round. He was looking sheepish. "How did you find out?"

"I saw the stamps in your passport. Why didn't you tell me you'd been in London?"

"I," he blushed. "I guess I acted stupidly. I was worried about Gina . . . and I didn't trust Garth. I followed them to London and then tried to do some amateur investigation of Garth's background. When I found out he had a fiancée and that no one seemed to know if she was still engaged to him or not, I called up Thérèse and arranged to meet her on Saturday evening. She didn't show up—since she was already dead by then—and after that I figured maybe I was making a fool of myself and it would be best if I went back to Paris. I got cold feet, I guess.

188

I didn't mention it to you because—well, I'd behaved stupidly, and—"

"I don't think it was stupid at all!" said Gina indignantly. "I think it was just wonderful of you to be concerned over me! When I think of all that trouble you went to—"

They gazed at each other in dizzy admiration, as if neither could believe the fairytale slice of good fortune which had befallen them. I began to feel distinctly *de trop*.

"Well," I began. "Now that that's all explained—"

The telephone rang. Gina, being nearest, picked up the receiver. "Hello? Oh, he*llo!* Is everything—yes, thank you. Yes. Who? *Claire?* Yes, she's right here. Just a moment." She turned to me in surprise. "It's Garth," she said, and added mystified: "He says he wants to speak to you. Do you suppose it's about some new development?"

"No," I said. "This development has been going on for at least four days." And I crossed the room towards the waiting telephone.

"I should have let Gina speak to you on the phone when you arrived in London," Garth said to me. "You had every right to be angry with me for not being honest with you and admitting I knew where she was, but the situation was so extraordinary and so dangerous that I was reluctant to involve you. It seemed to me that the less you knew the better. If you knew nothing I reasoned that you couldn't be a danger either to yourself or to us. But I was wrong."

It was Saturday night, exactly a week since I had been sitting in my Manhattan apartment and trying to trace Gina's call from Europe. Garth had taken me to dine at

189

a penthouse restaurant, and far below us, spread out in a panorama which seemed to stretch into infinity, lay the lights of London, the complex arteries of an enormous city pulsing with a life-force two thousand years old.

"Have you forgiven me yet for not being quite honest with you?"

"You were honest about the things that mattered. That's all that counts." I was feeling too starry-eyed to take issue.

"But you didn't believe me! Why are you so convinced I preferred Gina to you?"

"Was I?" How could I explain that I assumed every attractive man preferred Gina to me?

"Yes, you were! Now you're the one who's not being quite honest! You thought all along that my feeling for you was assumed and couldn't possibly be genuine—"

"Well, it all happened so suddenly! And you *had* been dating Gina!"

"A few casual evenings out in Paris to take my mind off Thérèse—"

"And you did travel to London with her!" Once I got started it was hard to let up—my schoolteacher logic, I guess.

"Thanks to careful engineering on her part—"

"And she ended up by living in your apartment, cooking your meals—"

"Let's say she tried to cook. I hope Warren's handy in the kitchen, otherwise they'll both starve. Incidentally, how's your cooking?"

Far below us the lights of London pricked the darkness with dazzling brilliance. A passing waiter paused long enough to refill our champagne glasses from the bottle in the ice bucket.

"Well," I said, "I do a very very classic soft-boiled egg."

"Really? Just right for breakfast." He raised his glass to me with a smile and his light eyes were no longer unreadable. "To your classic boiled eggs!" he said lightly. "And to the first opportunity I have to sample one!"

We were married three months later.

Sylvia Thorpe

Sparkling novels of love and conquest set against the colorful background of historic England. Here are stories you will savor word by word, page by page into the wee hours of the night.

☐ BEGGAR ON HORSEBACK	23091-0	1.50
☐ CAPTAIN GALLANT	Q2709	1.50
☐ FAIR SHINE THE DAY	23229-8	1.75
☐ THE GOLDEN PANTHER	23006-6	1.50
☐ THE RELUCTANT ADVENTURESS	P2578	1.25
☐ ROGUE'S COVENANT	23041-4	1.50
☐ ROMANTIC LADY	Q2910	1.50
☐ THE SCANDALOUS LADY ROBIN	Q2934	1.50
☐ THE SCAPEGRACE	P2663	1.25
☐ THE SCARLET DOMINO	23220-4	1.50
☐ THE SILVER NIGHTINGALE	P2626	1.25
☐ THE SWORD AND THE SHADOW	22945-9	1.50
☐ SWORD OF VENGEANCE	23136-4	1.50
☐ TARRINGTON CHASE	Q2843	1.50